BENNY AND PENNY

IN

LOST AND FOUND!

PENNY!

A TOON BOOK BY

GEOFFREY HAYES

TOON BOOKS • NEW YORK

A JUNIOR LIBRARY GUILD SELECTION

KIRKUS BEST CONTINUING SERIES

Make sure to find all the Benny and Penny books:
Benny and Penny in Just Pretend
Benny and Penny in The Big No-No!, **A GEISEL AWARD WINNER!**
Benny and Penny in The Toy Breaker
Benny and Penny in Lost and Found
Benny and Penny in Lights Out!
Benny and Penny in How to Say Goodbye

Editorial Director: FRANÇOISE MOULY

Book Design: FRANÇOISE MOULY & JONATHAN BENNETT

GEOFFREY HAYES' artwork was done in colored pencil.

A TOON Book™ © 2014 Geoffrey Hayes & & TOON Books, an imprint of Raw Junior, LLC, 27 Greene Street, New York, NY 10013. No part of this book may be used or reproduced in any manner whatsoever without written permission except in the case of brief quotations embodied in critical articles and reviews. TOON Graphics™, TOON Books®, LITTLE LIT® and TOON Into Reading!™ are trademarks of RAW Junior, LLC. All rights reserved. Library of Congress Cataloging-in-Publication Data: Hayes, Geoffrey. Benny and Penny in Lost and found : a TOON book / by Geoffrey Hayes. pages cm. –(Easy-to-read comics. Level 2) SUMMARY: Penny the mouse tries to help her brother Benny find his favorite hat, but Benny warns her that he is in a bad mood. ISBN 978-1-935179-64-1(hardcover) 1. Graphic novels. [1. Graphic novels. 2. Lost and found possessions--Fiction. 3. Mood (Psychology)--Fiction. 4. Brothers and sisters--Fiction. 5. Mice--Fiction.] I. Title. II. Title: Lost and found. PZ7.7.H39Bd 2014 741.5'973--dc23 2014000649 All our books are Smyth Sewn (the highest library-quality binding available) and printed with soy-based inks on acid-free, woodfree paper harvested from responsible sources. Printed in China by C&C Offset Printing Co., Ltd.

Distributed to the trade by Consortium Book Sales & Distribution, a division of Ingram Content Group; orders (866) 400-5351; ips@ingramcontent.com; www.cbsd.com.

ISBN 978-1-935179-64-1 (hardcover)   ISBN 978-1-943145-50-8 (softcover)

19 20 21 22 23 24 C&C 10 9 8 7 6 5 4 3 2

WWW.TOON-BOOKS.COM

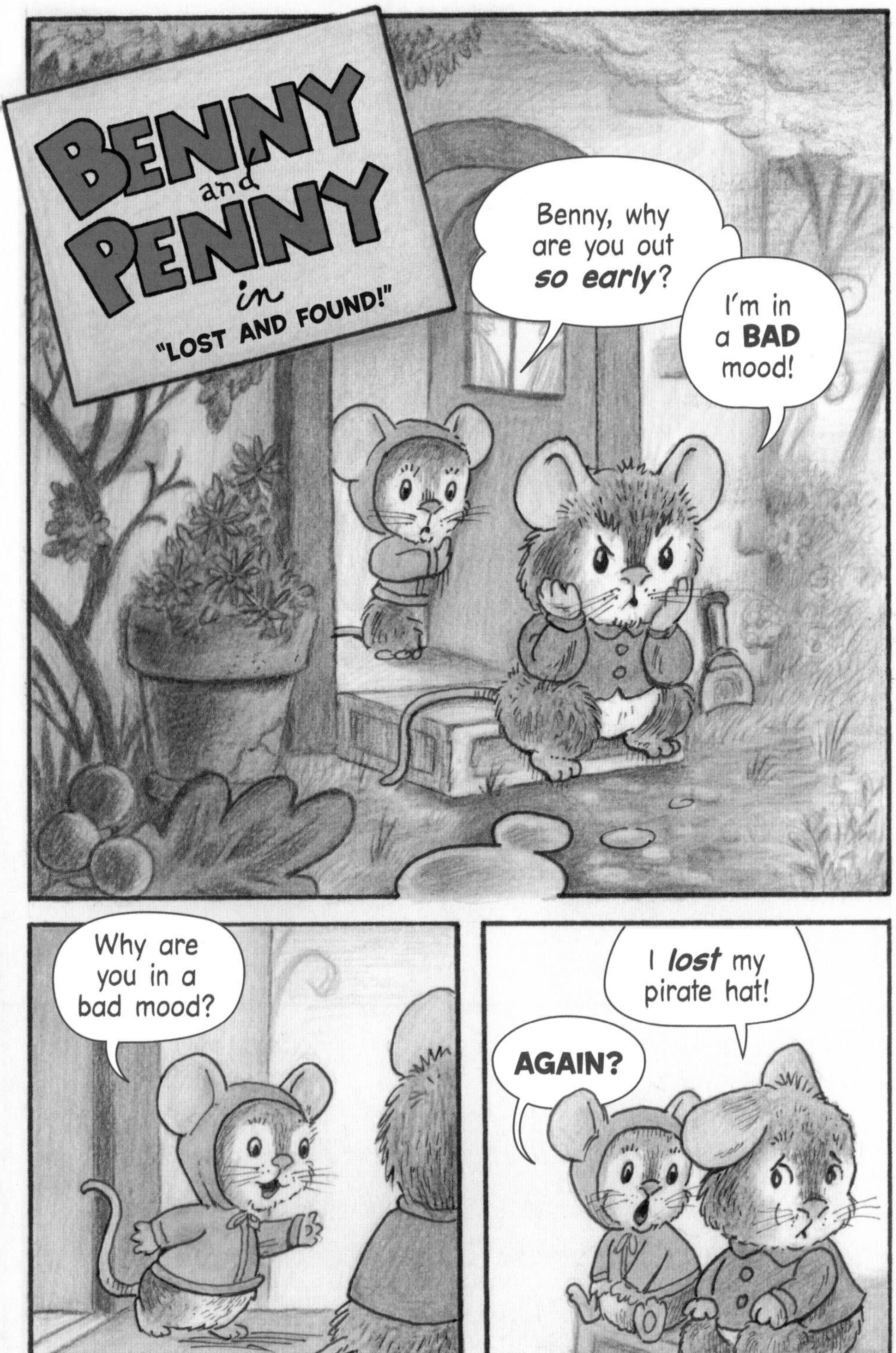
BENNY and PENNY
in
"LOST AND FOUND!"
Benny, why are you out *so early*?
I'm in a **BAD** mood!
Why are you in a bad mood?
I *lost* my pirate hat!
AGAIN?

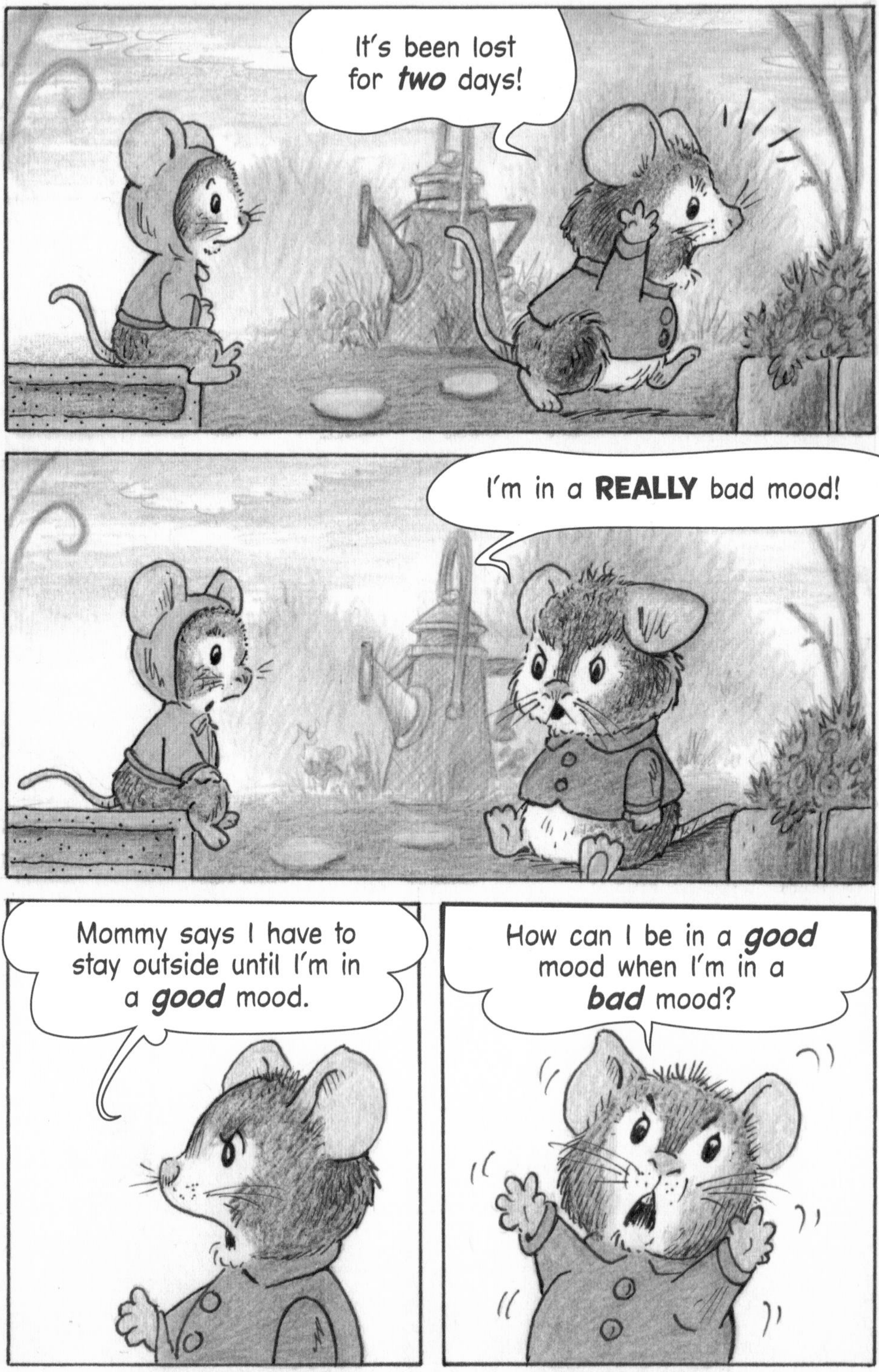
It's been lost for *two* days!
I'm in a **REALLY** bad mood!
Mommy says I have to stay outside until I'm in a *good* mood.
How can I be in a *good* mood when I'm in a *bad* mood?

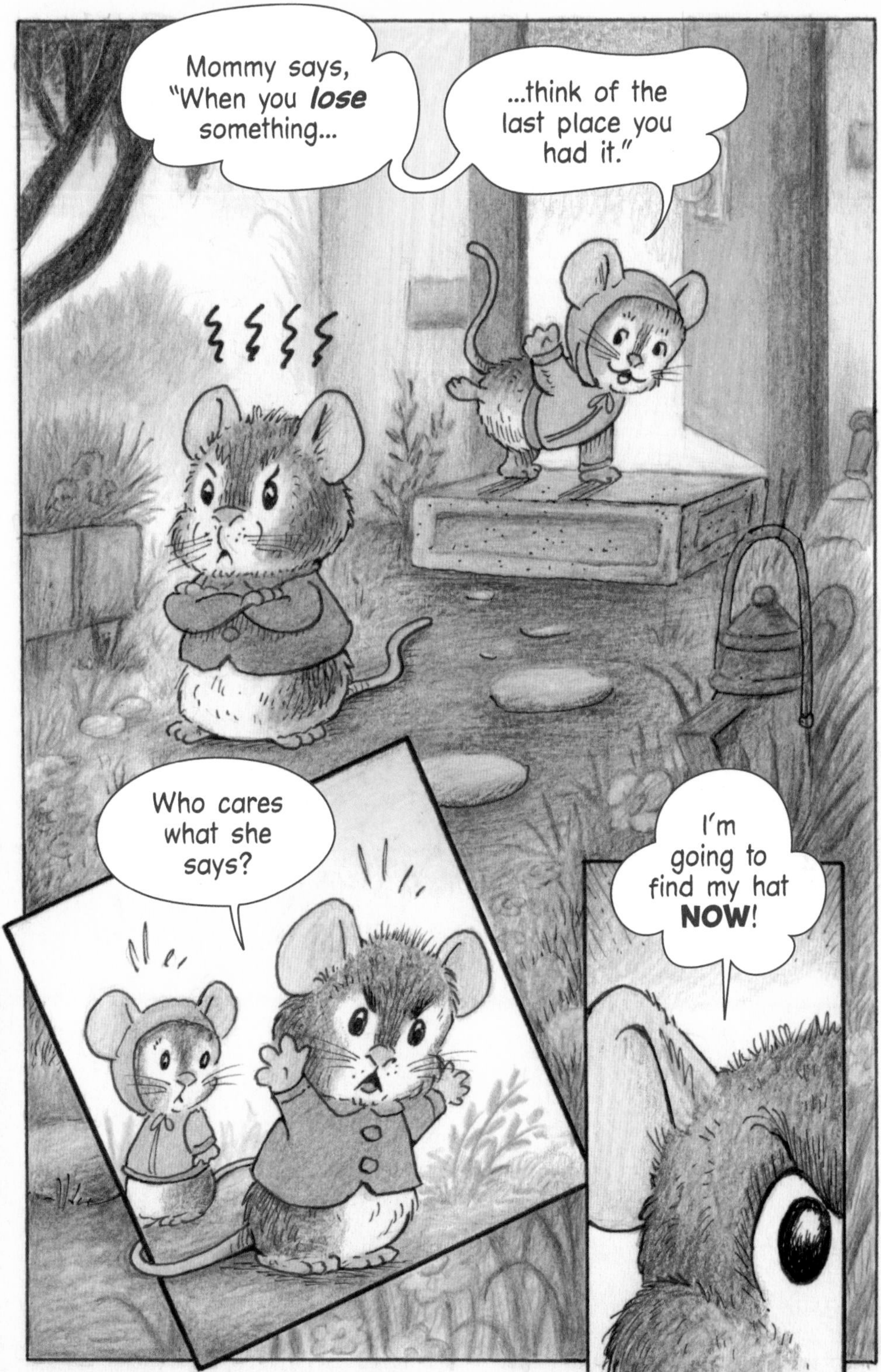
Mommy says, "When you ***lose*** something...
...think of the last place you had it."
Who cares what she says?
I'm going to find my hat **NOW**!

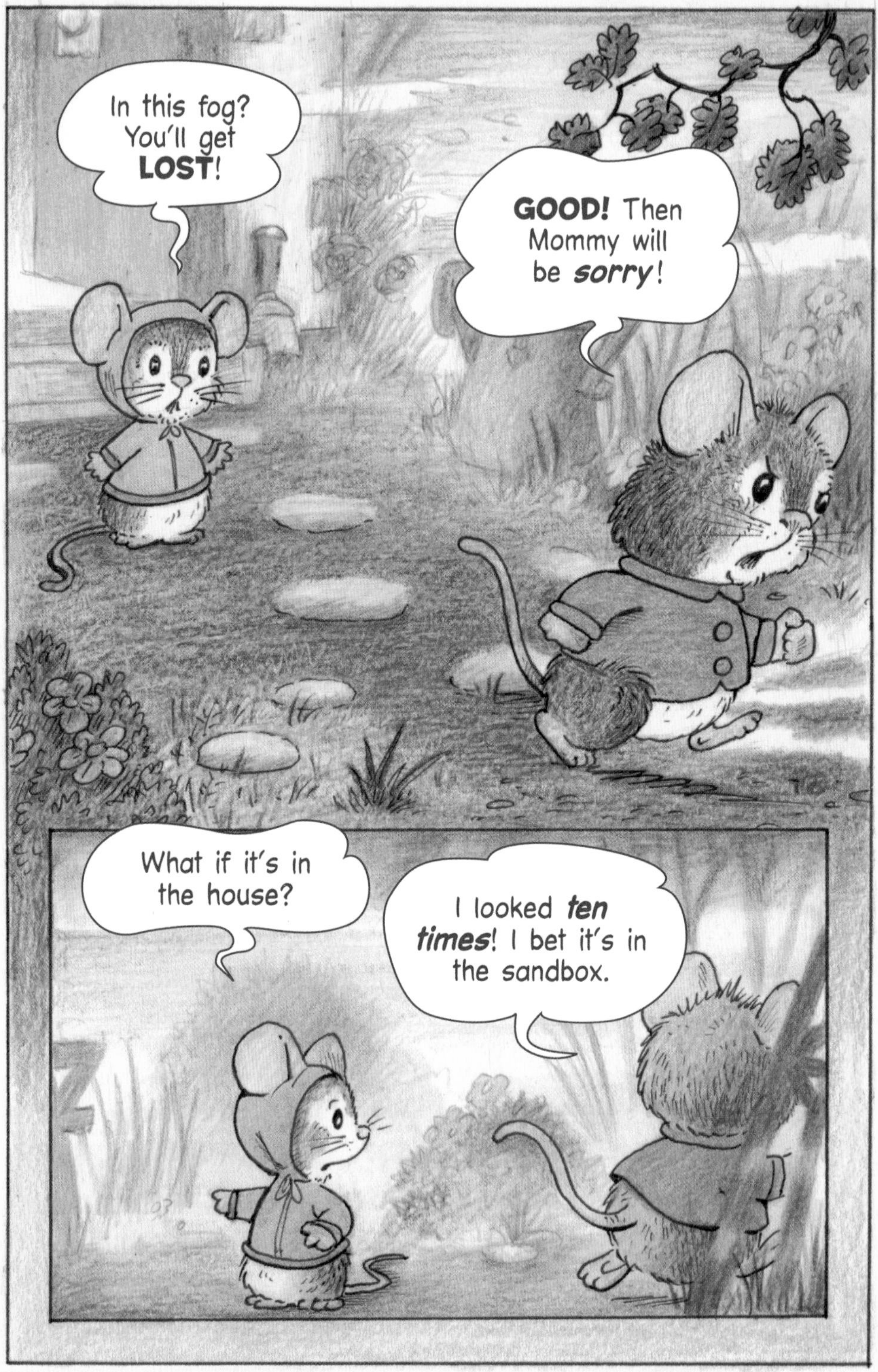
In this fog? You'll get **LOST**!
GOOD! Then Mommy will be ***sorry***!
What if it's in the house?
I looked ***ten times***! I bet it's in the sandbox.

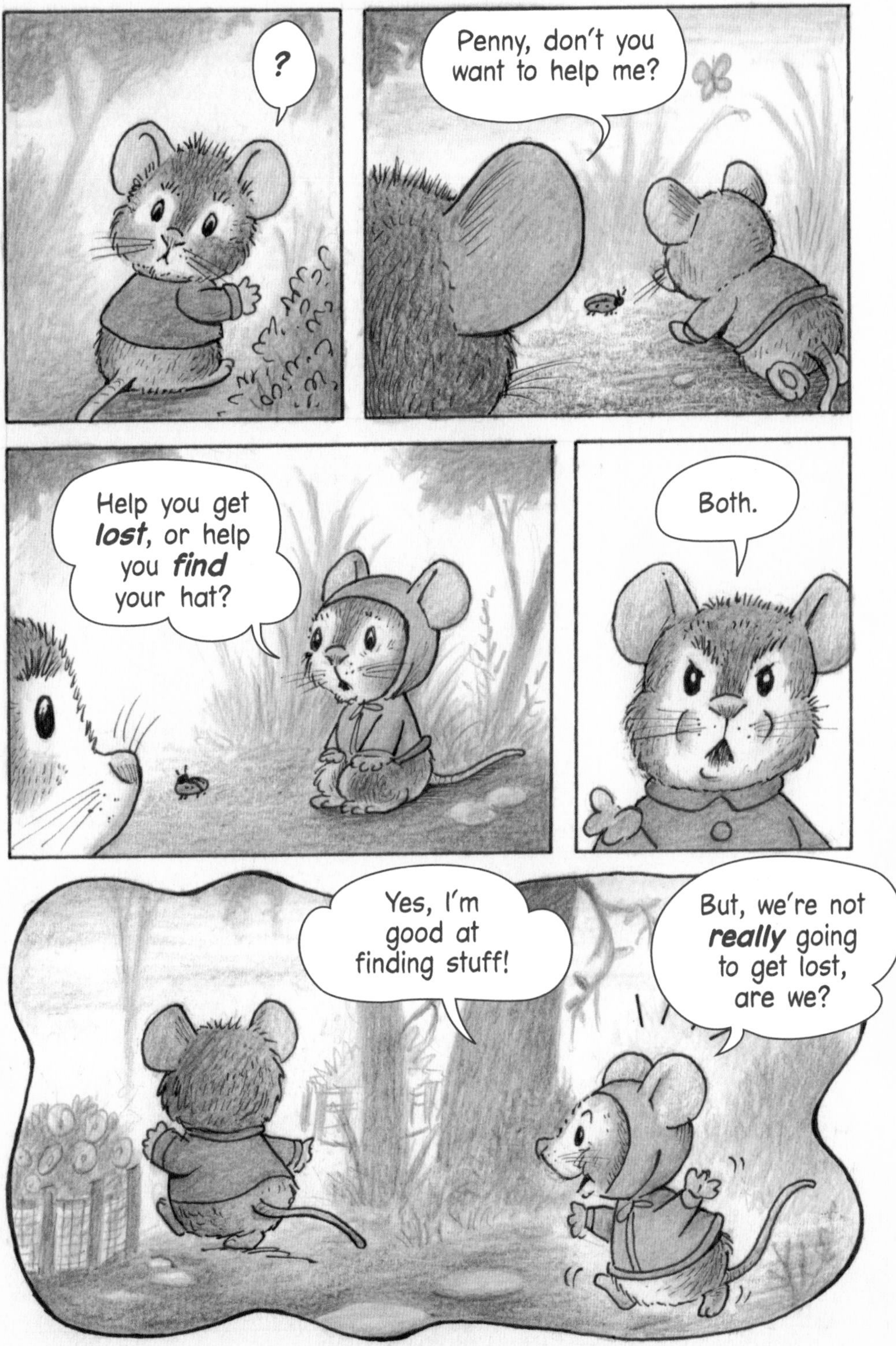
?
Penny, don't you want to help me?
Help you get ***lost***, or help you ***find*** your hat?
Both.
Yes, I'm good at finding stuff!
But, we're not ***really*** going to get lost, are we?

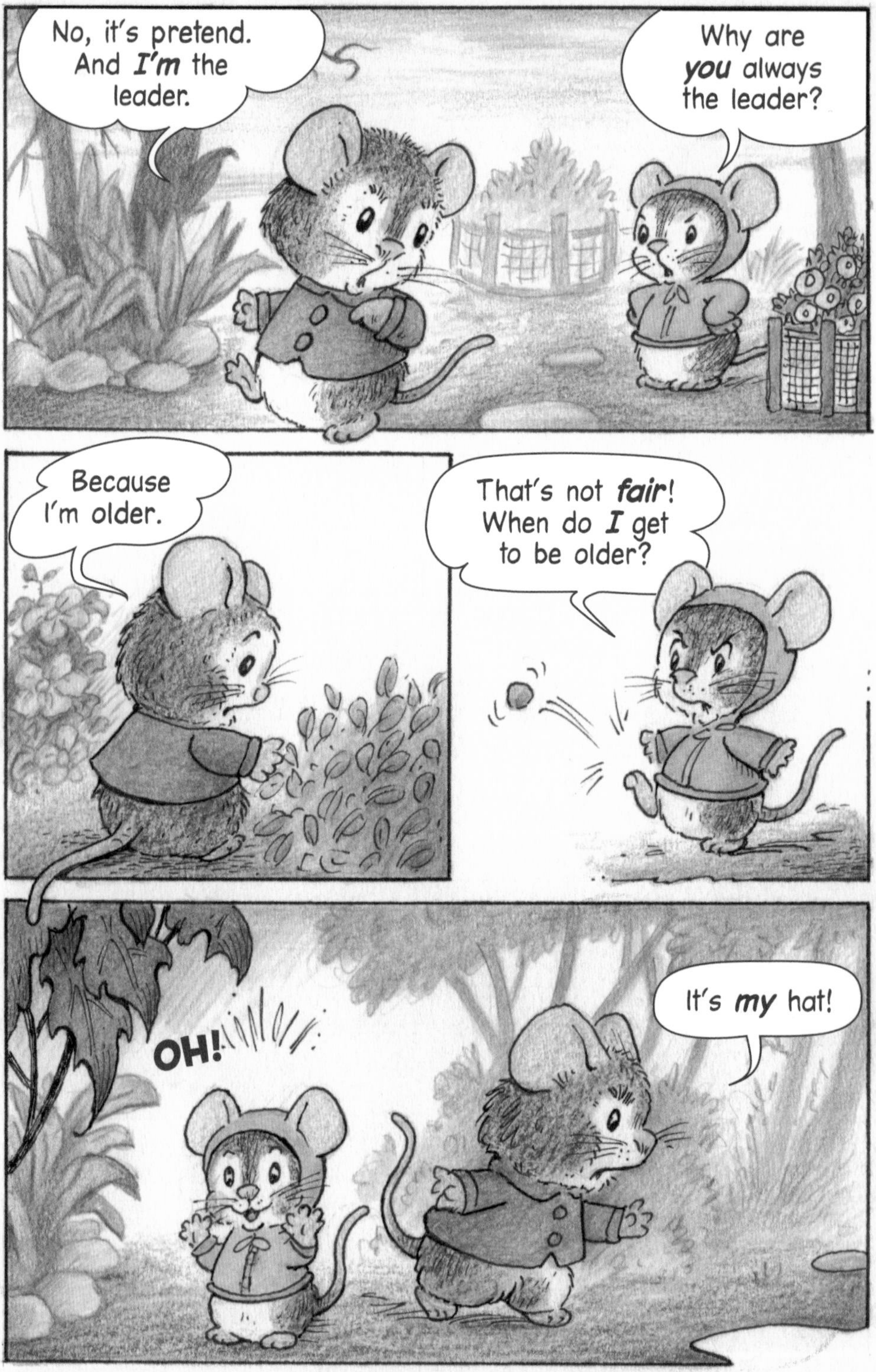
No, it's pretend. And *I'm* the leader.
Why are *you* always the leader?
Because I'm older.
That's not *fair*! When do *I* get to be older?
OH!
It's *my* hat!

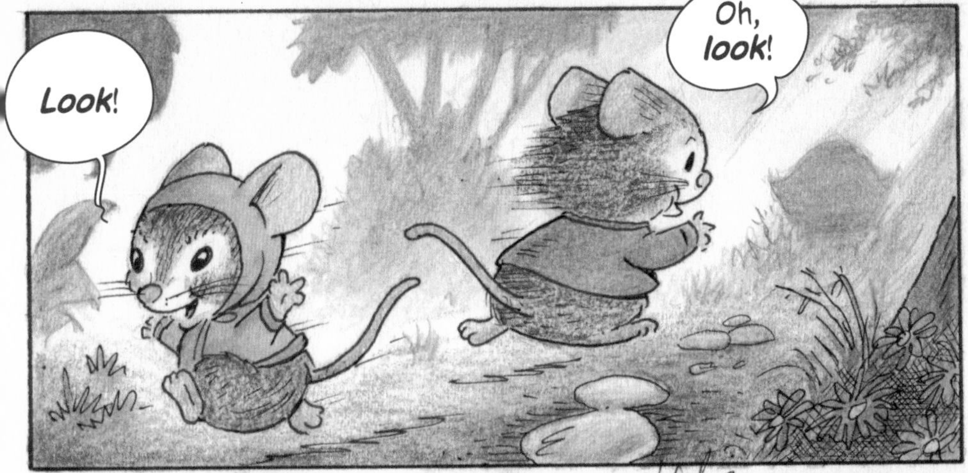
Look!
Oh, look!

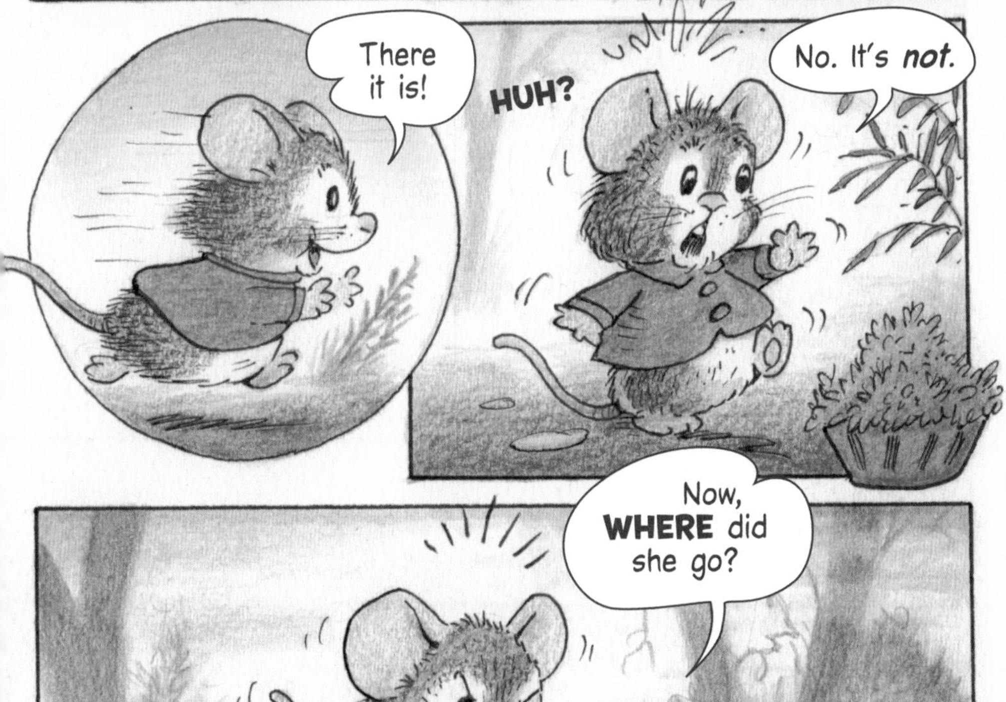
There it is!
HUH?
No. It's not.

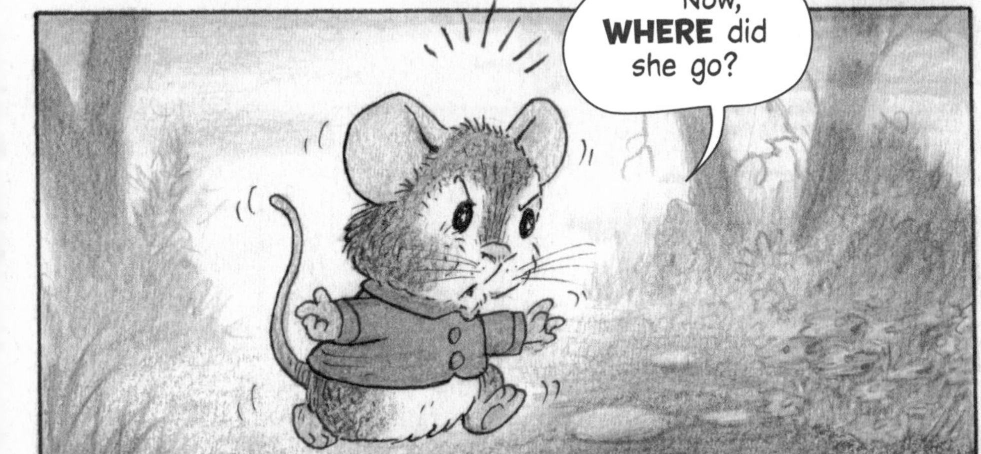
Now, WHERE did she go?

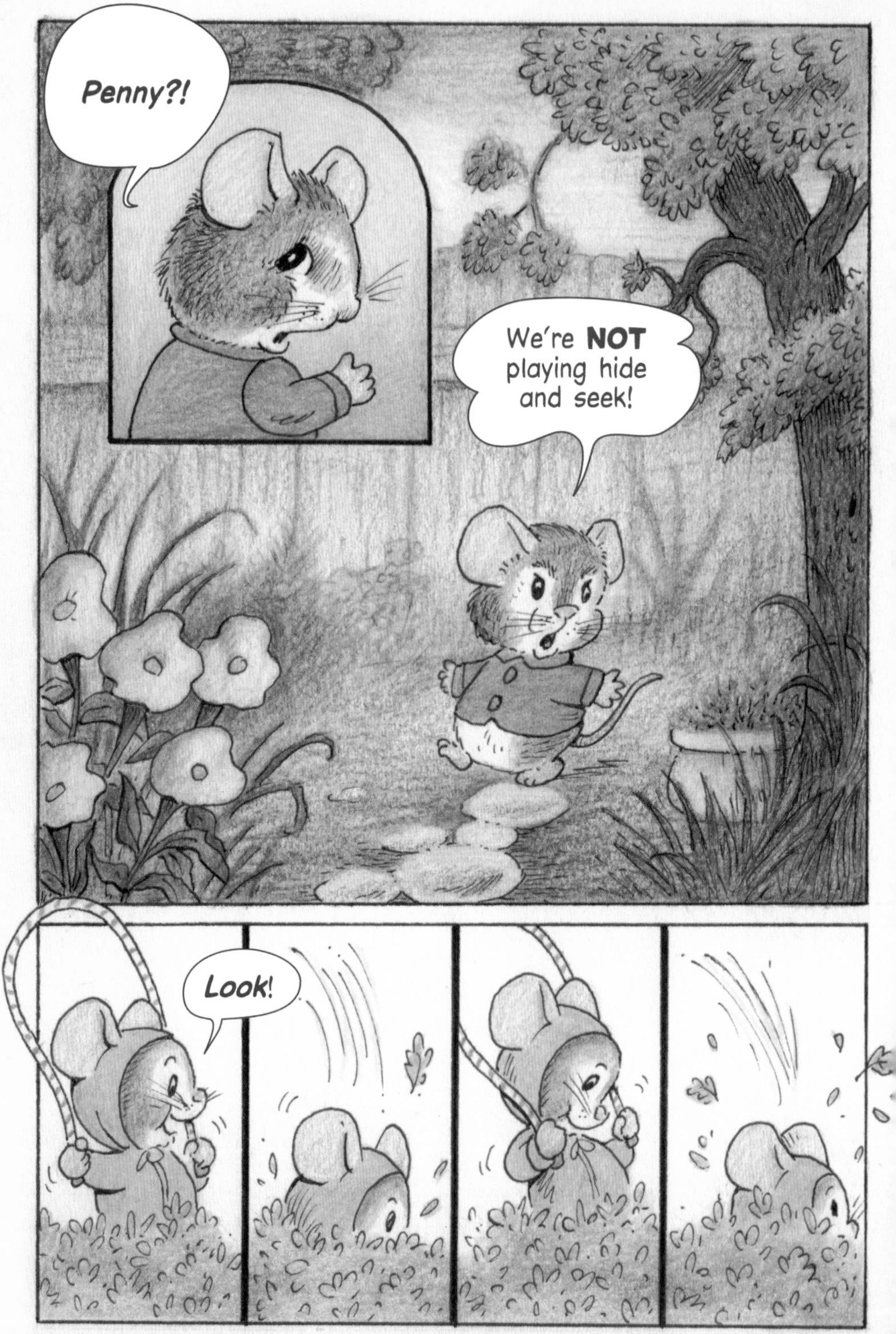
Penny?!
We're **NOT** playing hide and seek!
Look!

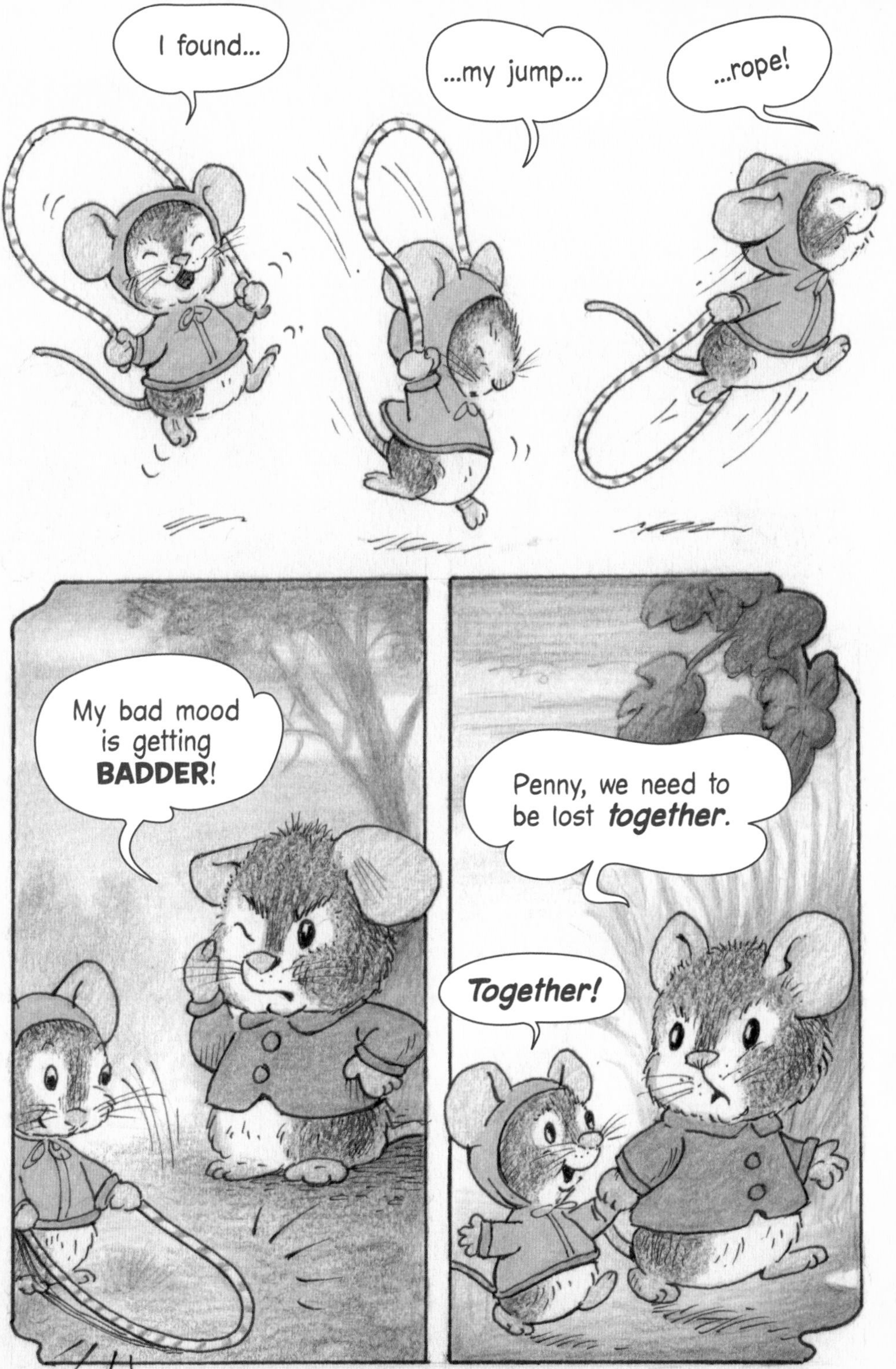
I found...
...my jump...
...rope!
My bad mood is getting **BADDER**!
Penny, we need to be lost ***together***.
Together!

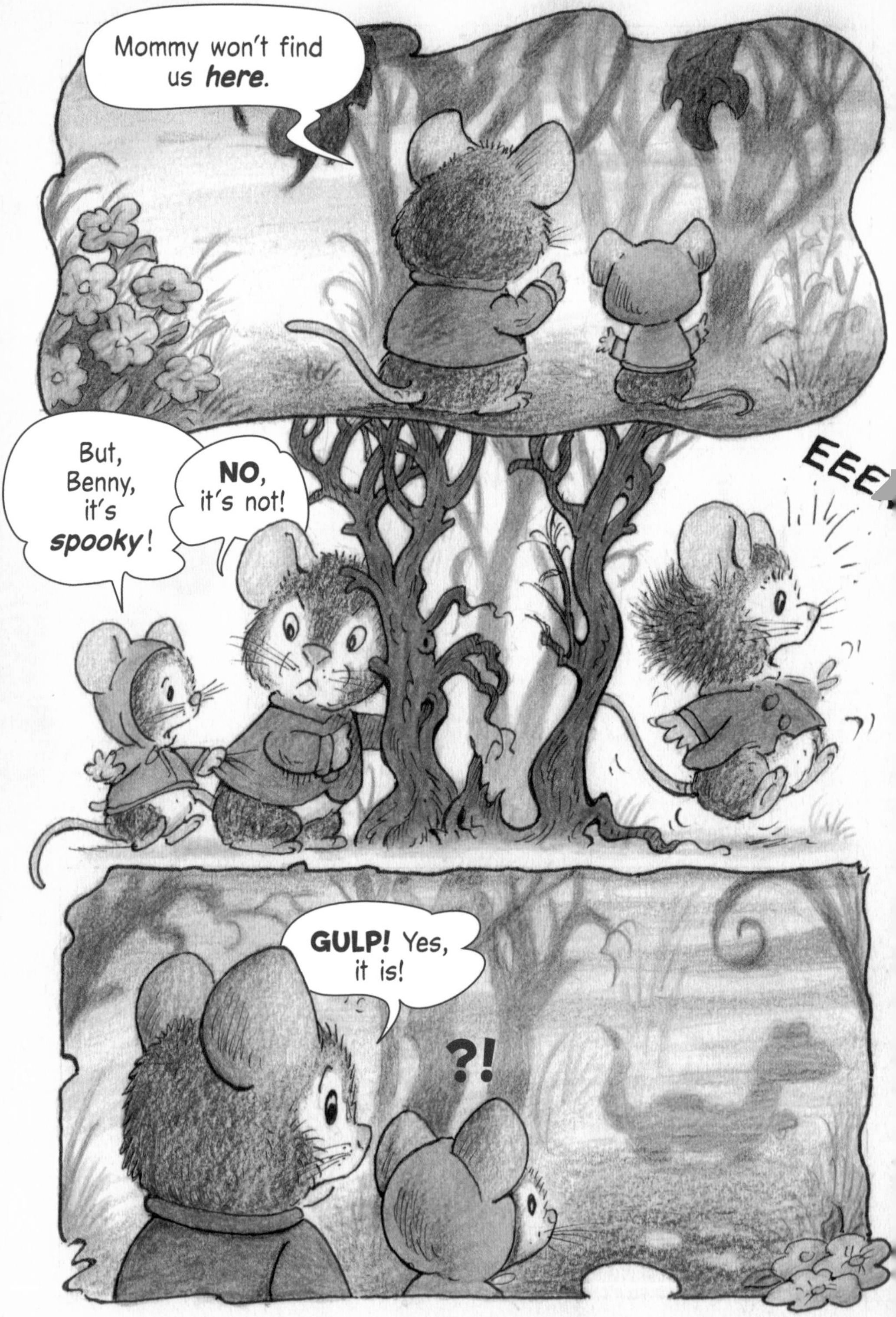

Mommy won't find us *here*.
But, Benny, it's *spooky*!
NO, it's not!
EEE
GULP! Yes, it is!
?!

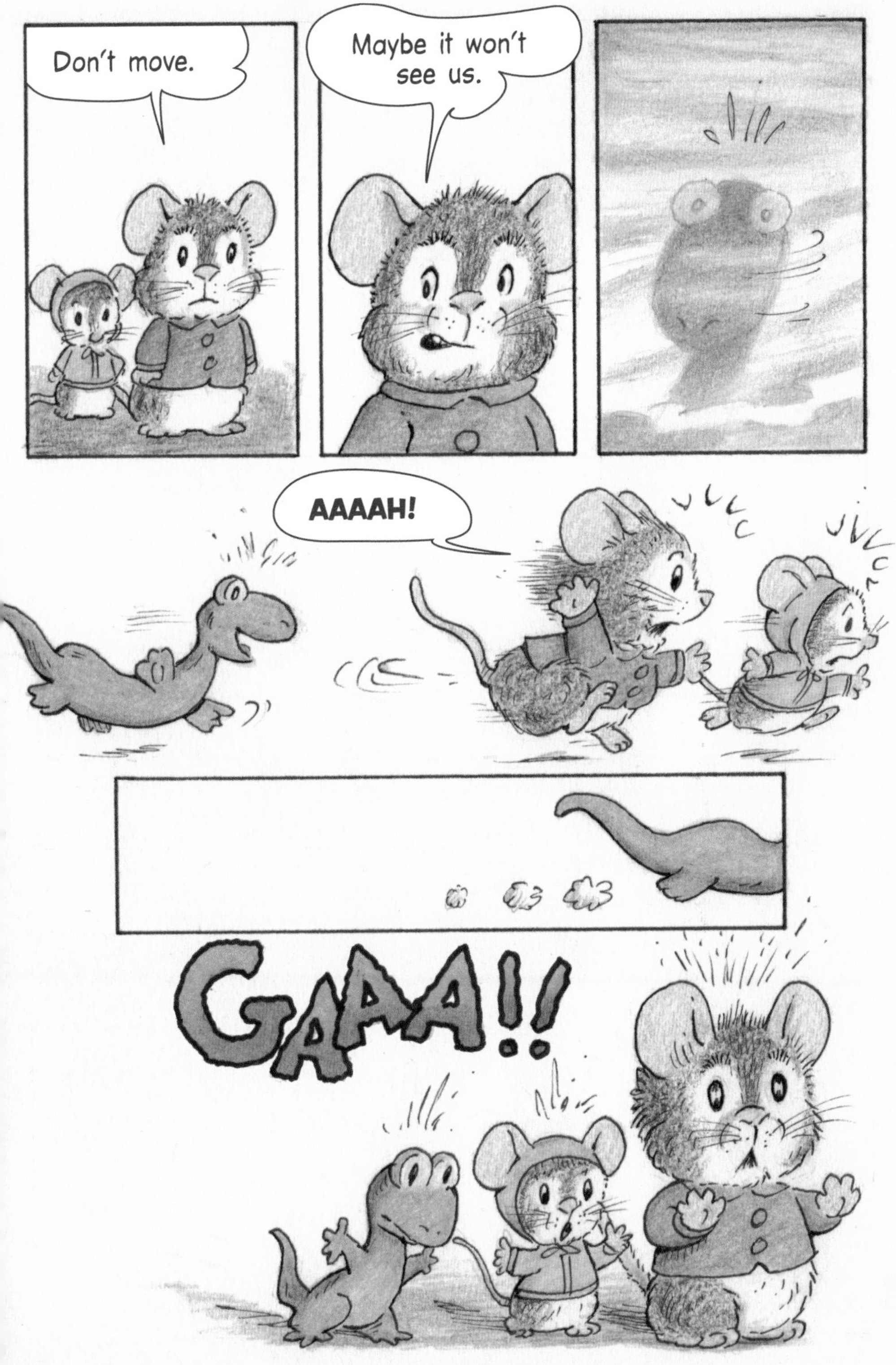
Don't move.
Maybe it won't see us.
AAAAH!
GAAA!!

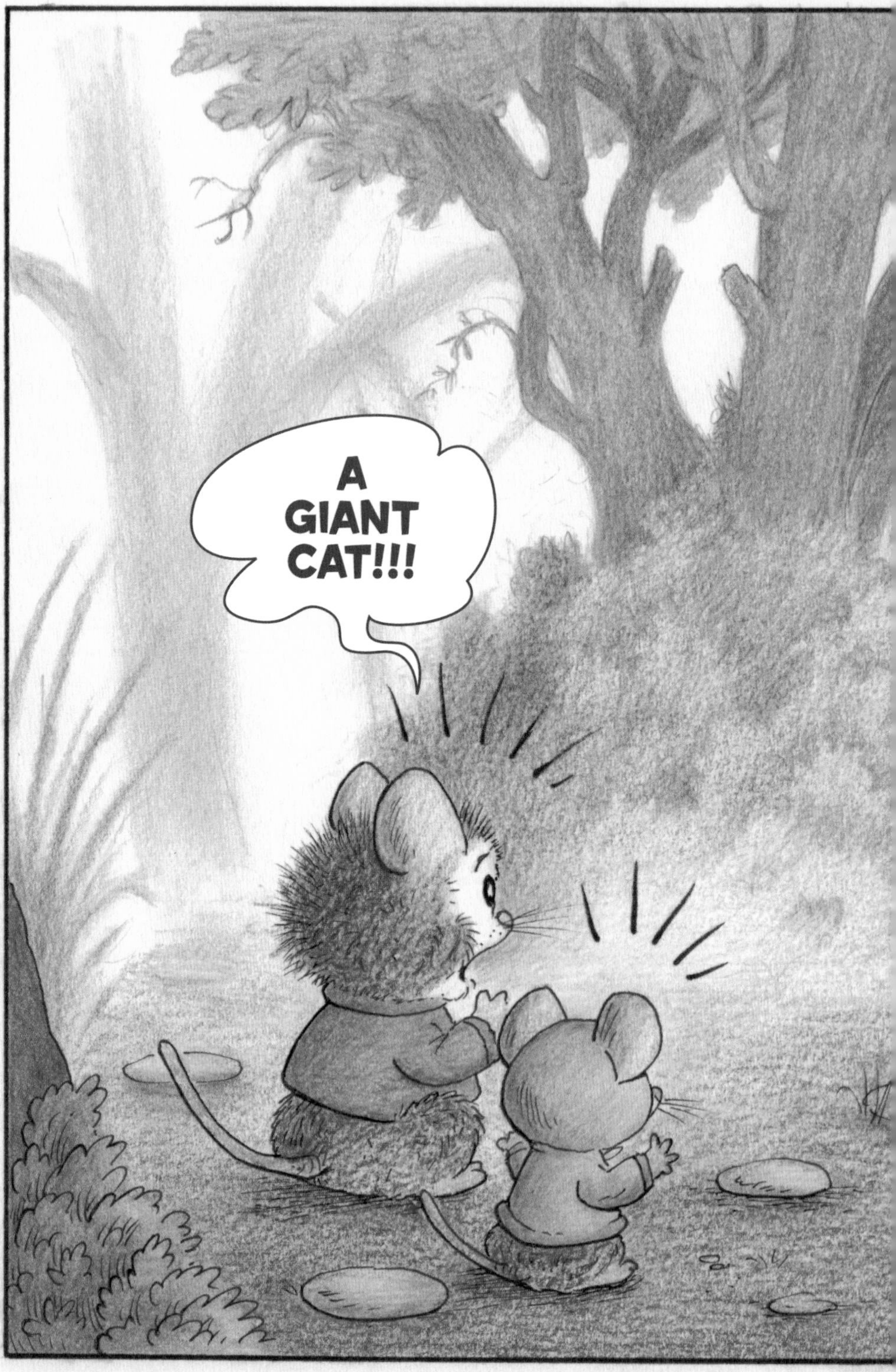
A GIANT CAT!!!

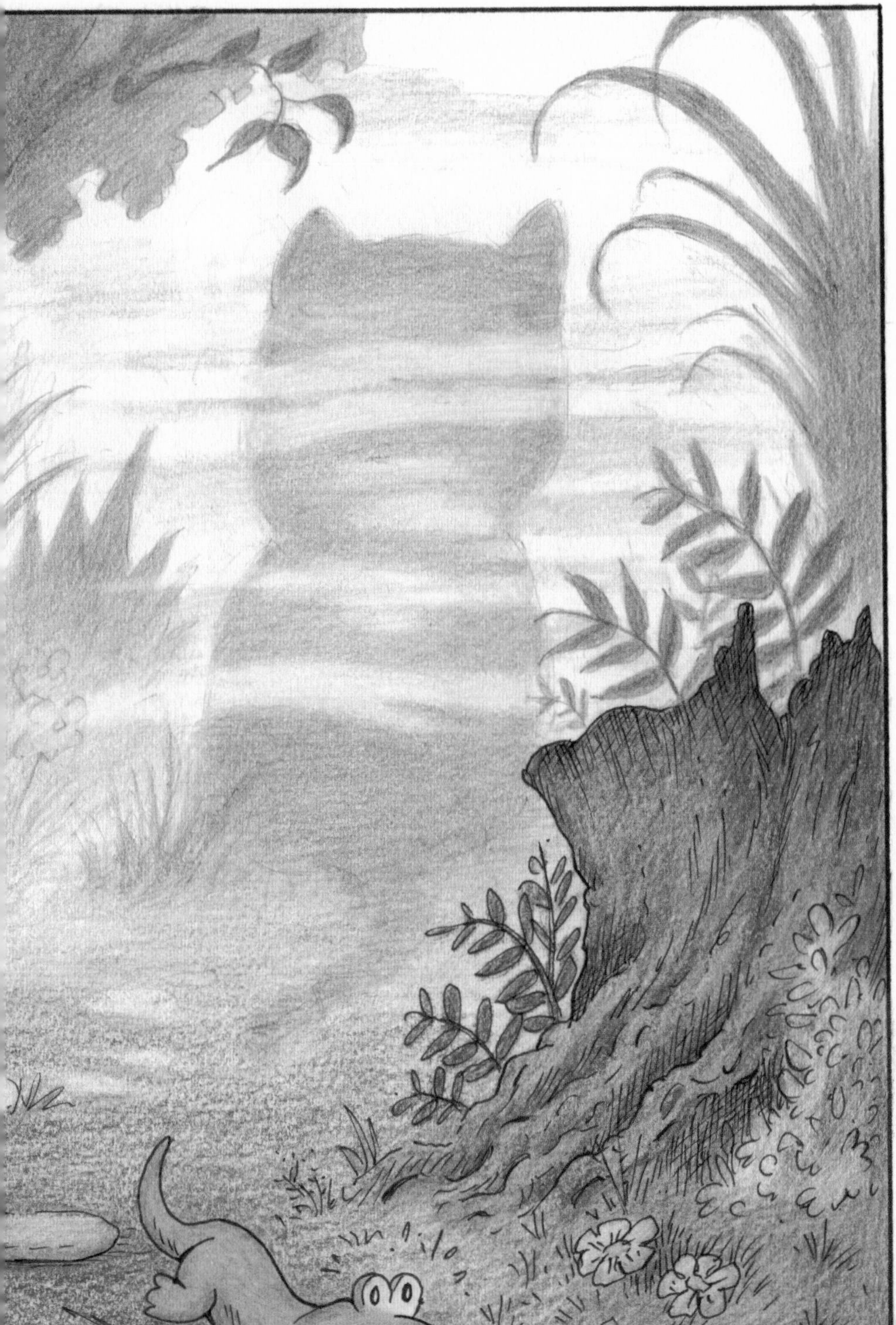

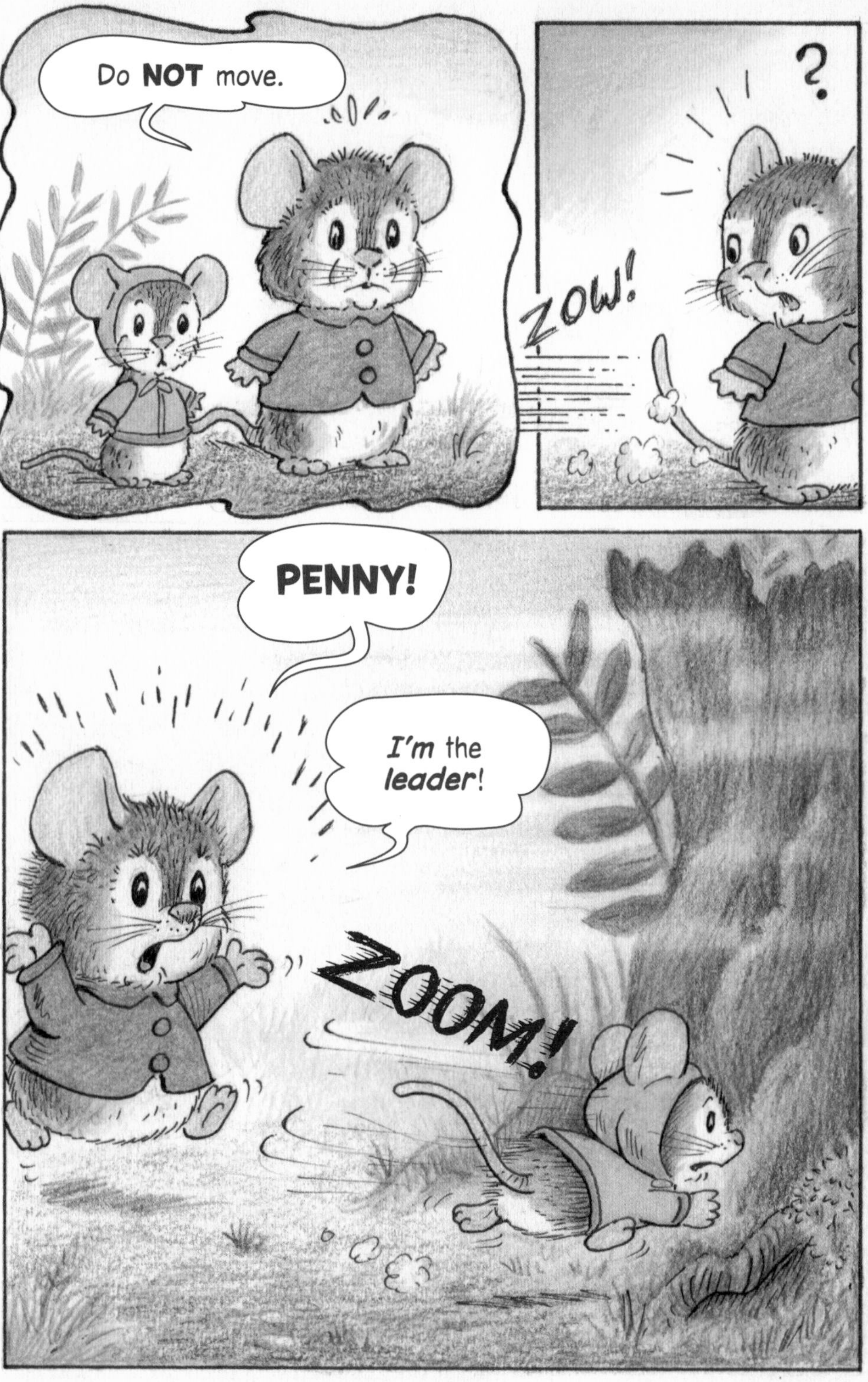
Do NOT move.
?
ZOW!
PENNY!
I'm the leader!
ZOOM!

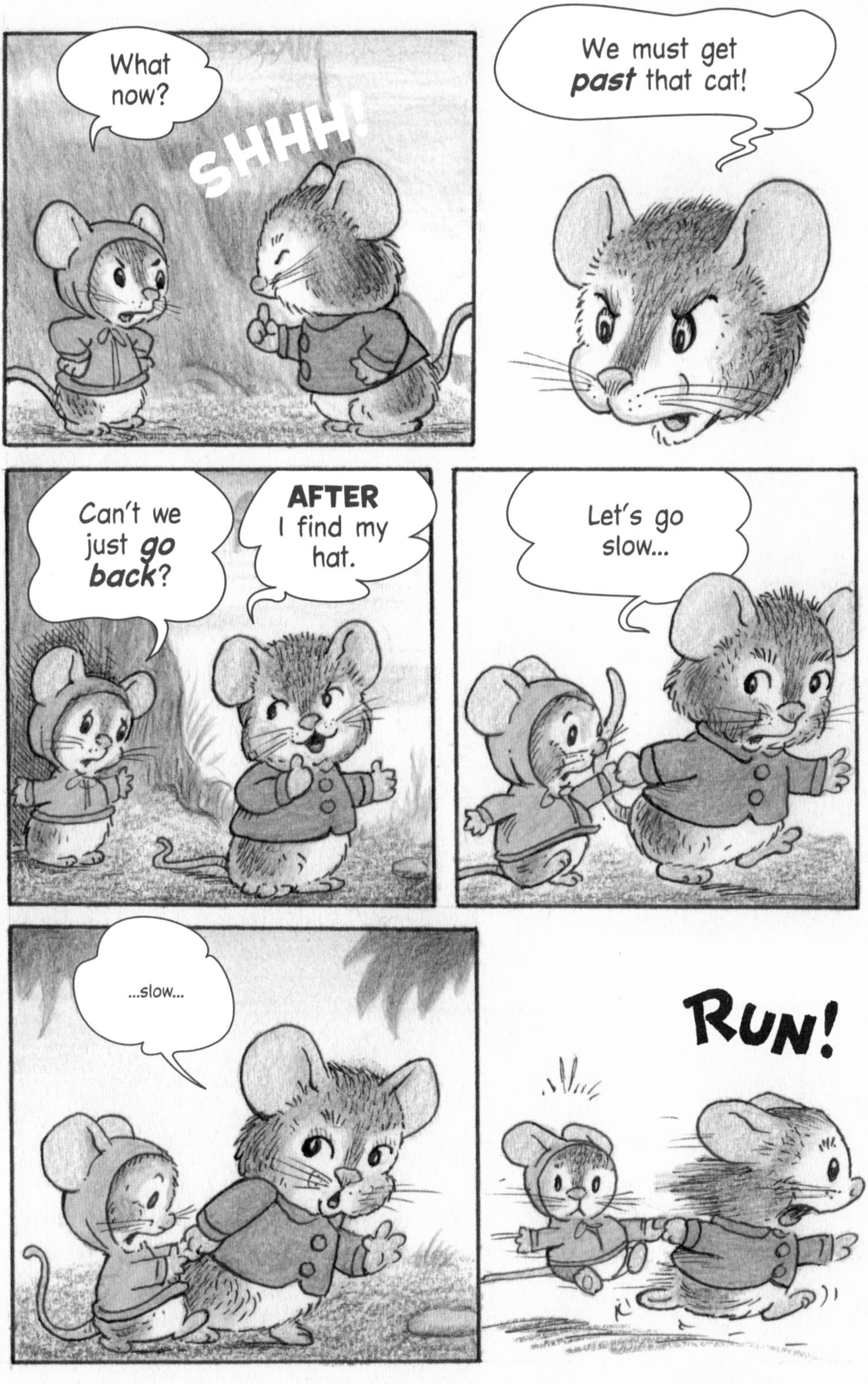
What now?
SHHH!
We must get *past* that cat!
Can't we just *go back*?
AFTER I find my hat.
Let's go slow...
...slow...
RUN!

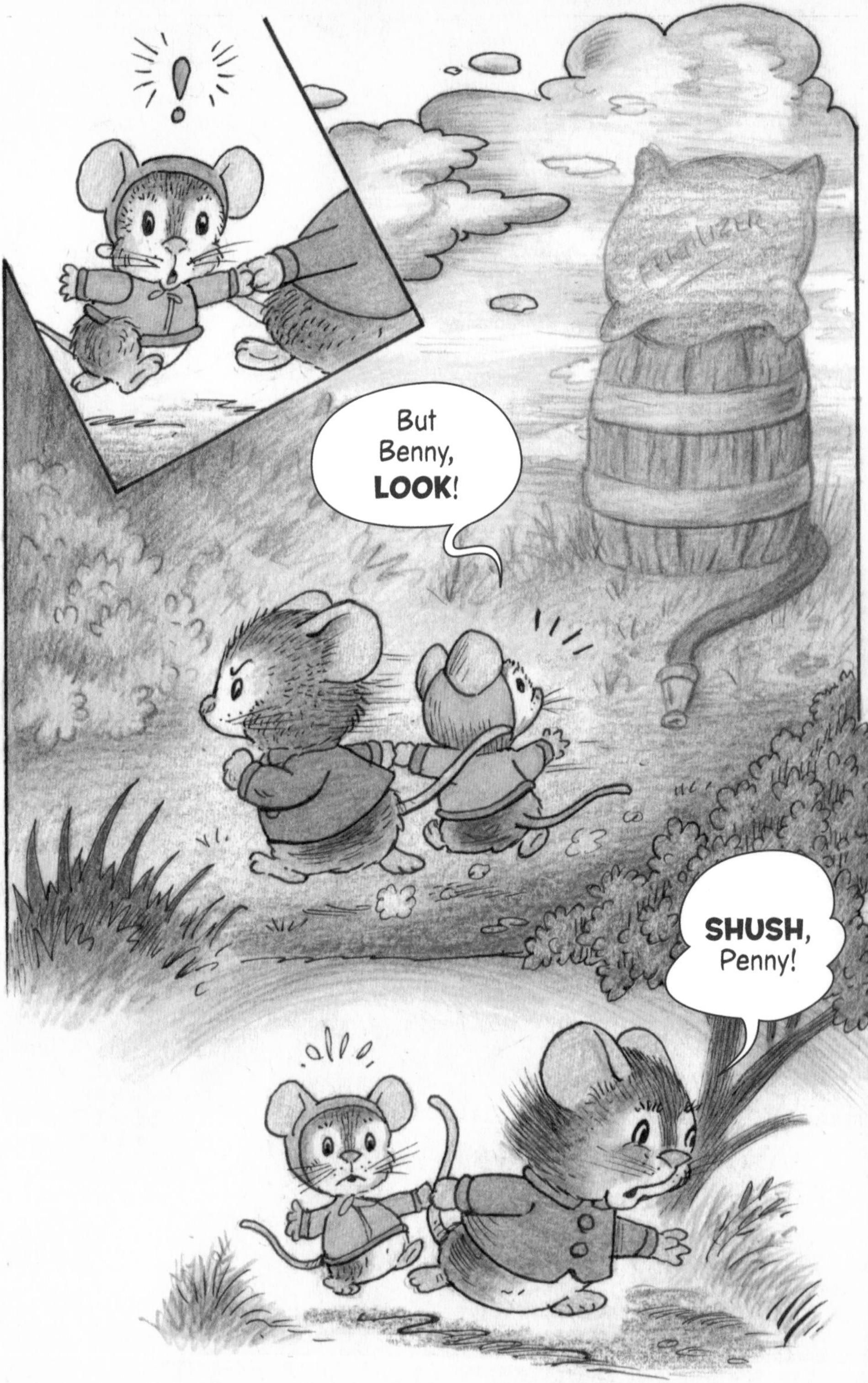
But Benny, **LOOK**!
SHUSH, Penny!

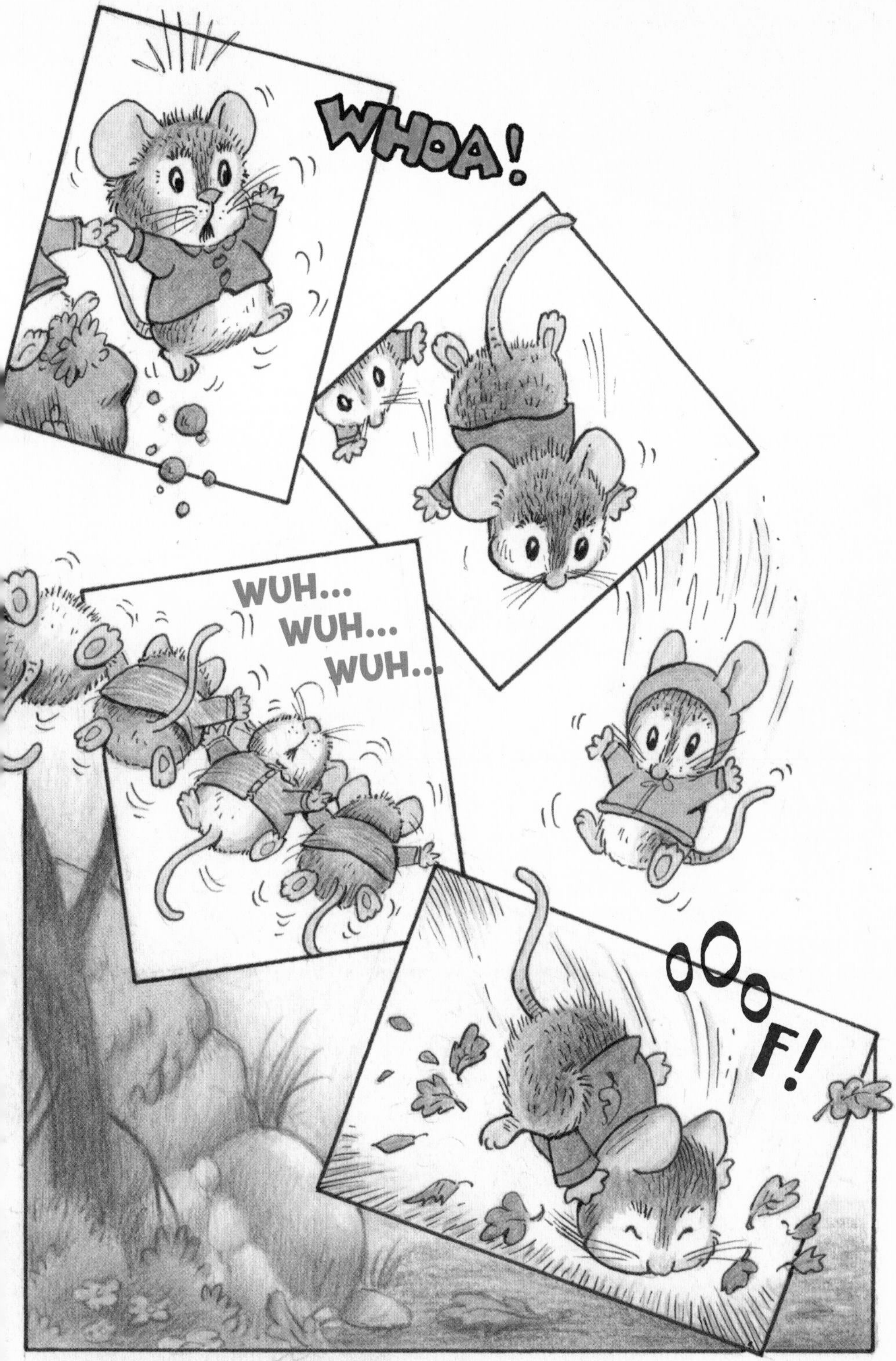
WHOA!
WUH... WUH... WUH...
OOOF!

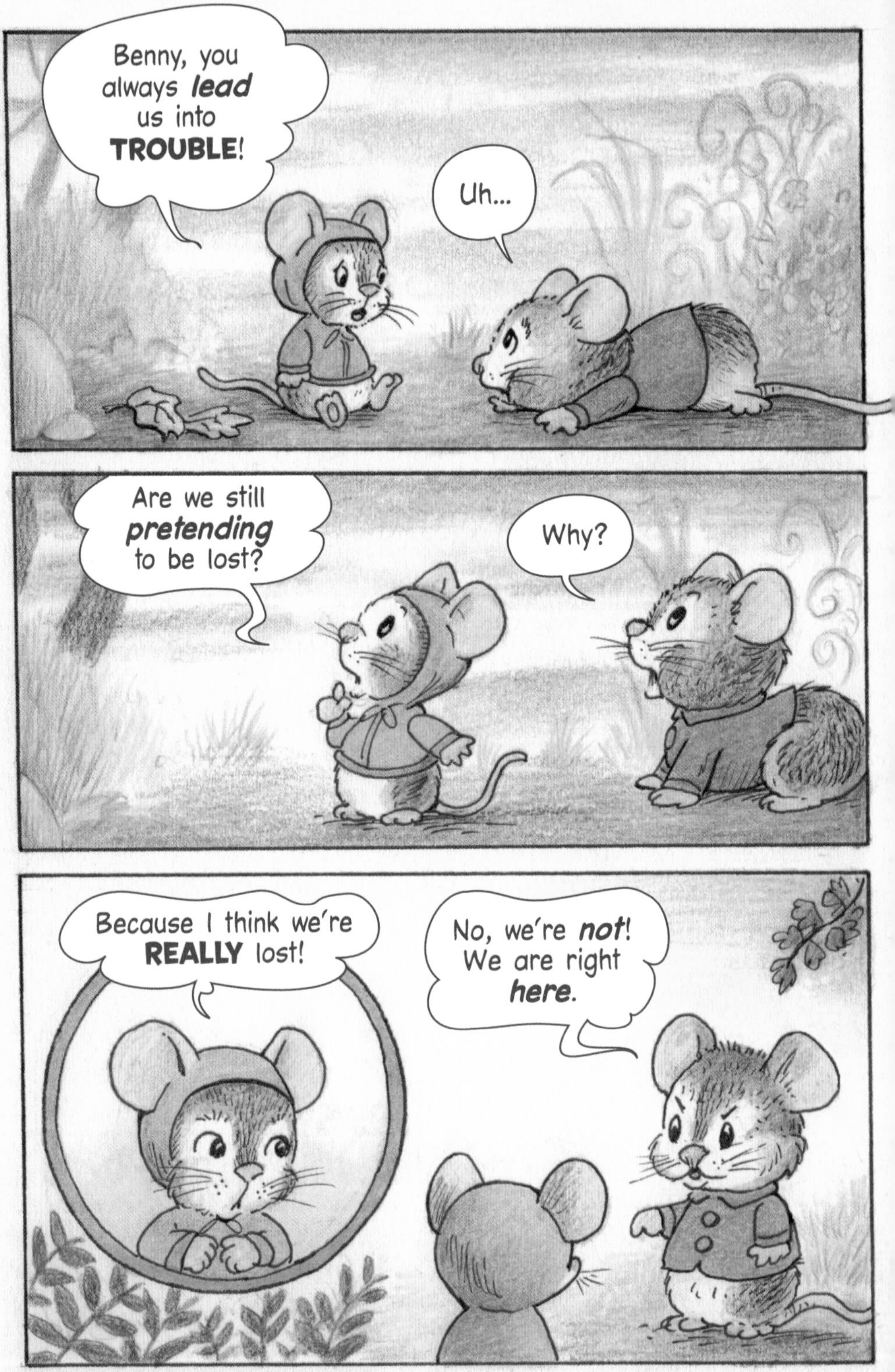

Benny, you always *lead* us into **TROUBLE**!
Uh...
Are we still *pretending* to be lost?
Why?
Because I think we're **REALLY** lost!
No, we're *not*! We are right *here*.

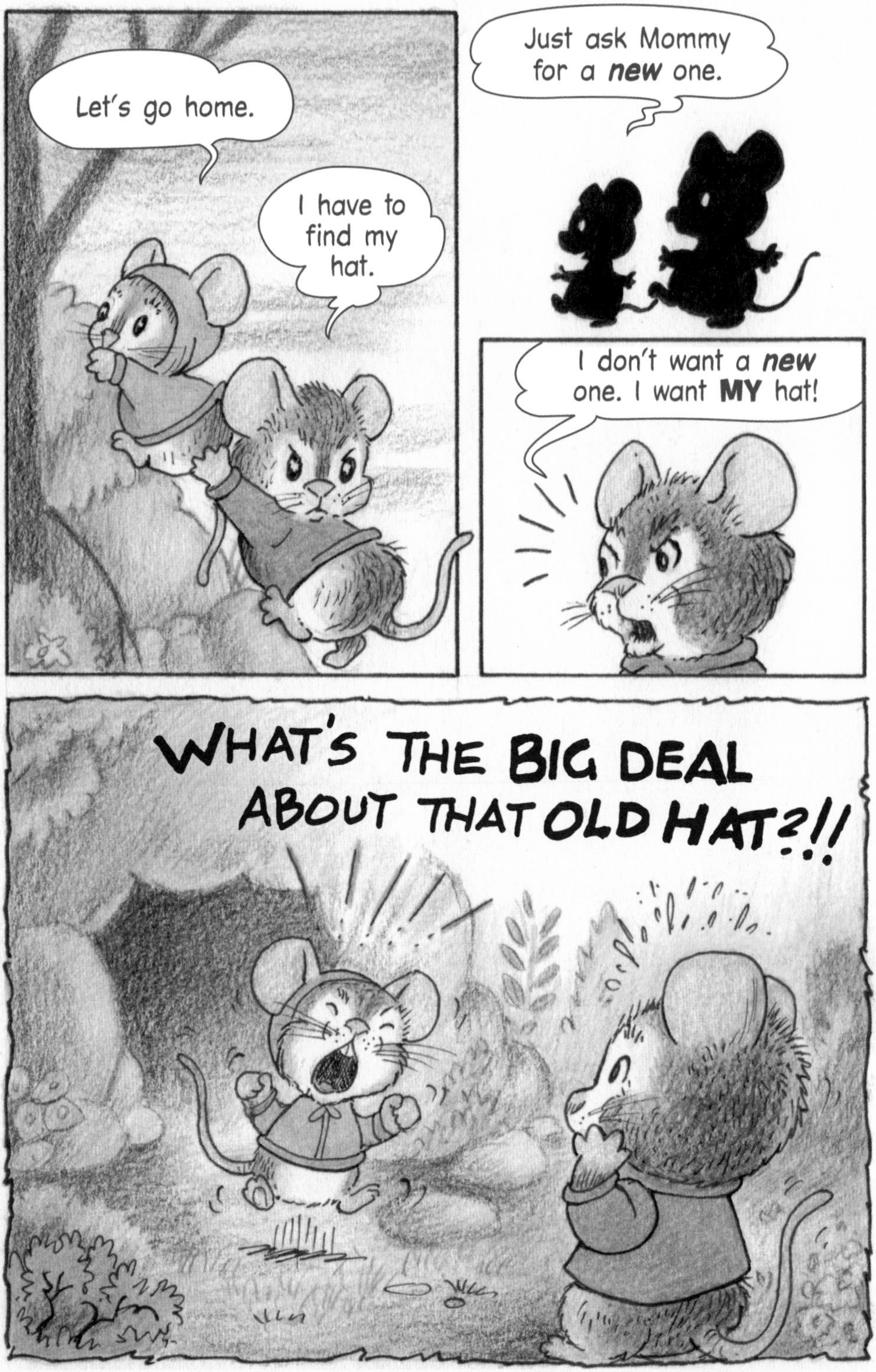
Let's go home.
I have to find my hat.
Just ask Mommy for a **new** one.
I don't want a **new** one. I want **MY** hat!
WHAT'S THE BIG DEAL ABOUT THAT OLD HAT?!!

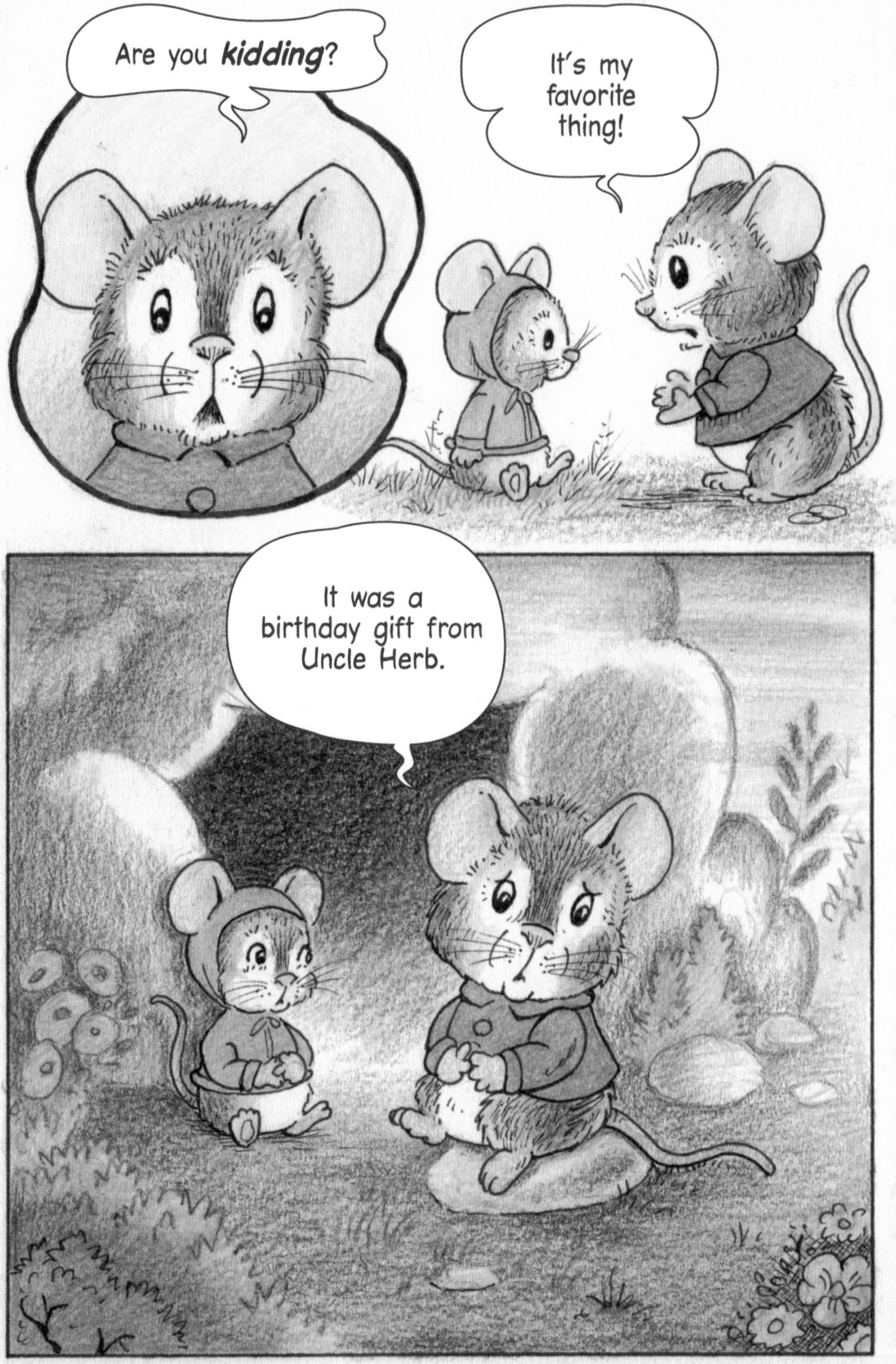
Are you ***kidding***?
It's my favorite thing!
It was a birthday gift from Uncle Herb.

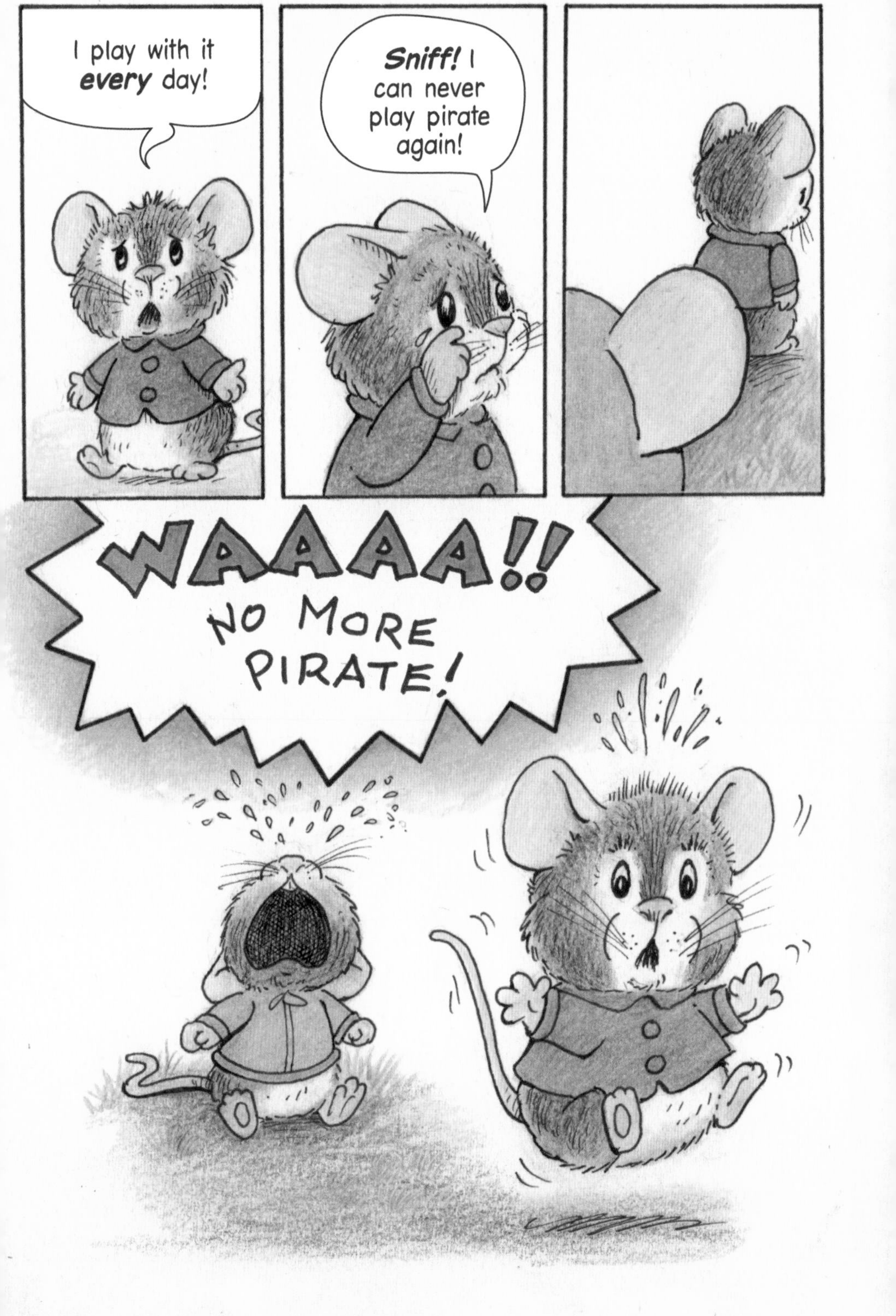
I play with it **every** day!
Sniff! I can never play pirate again!
WAAAA!!
NO MORE PIRATE!

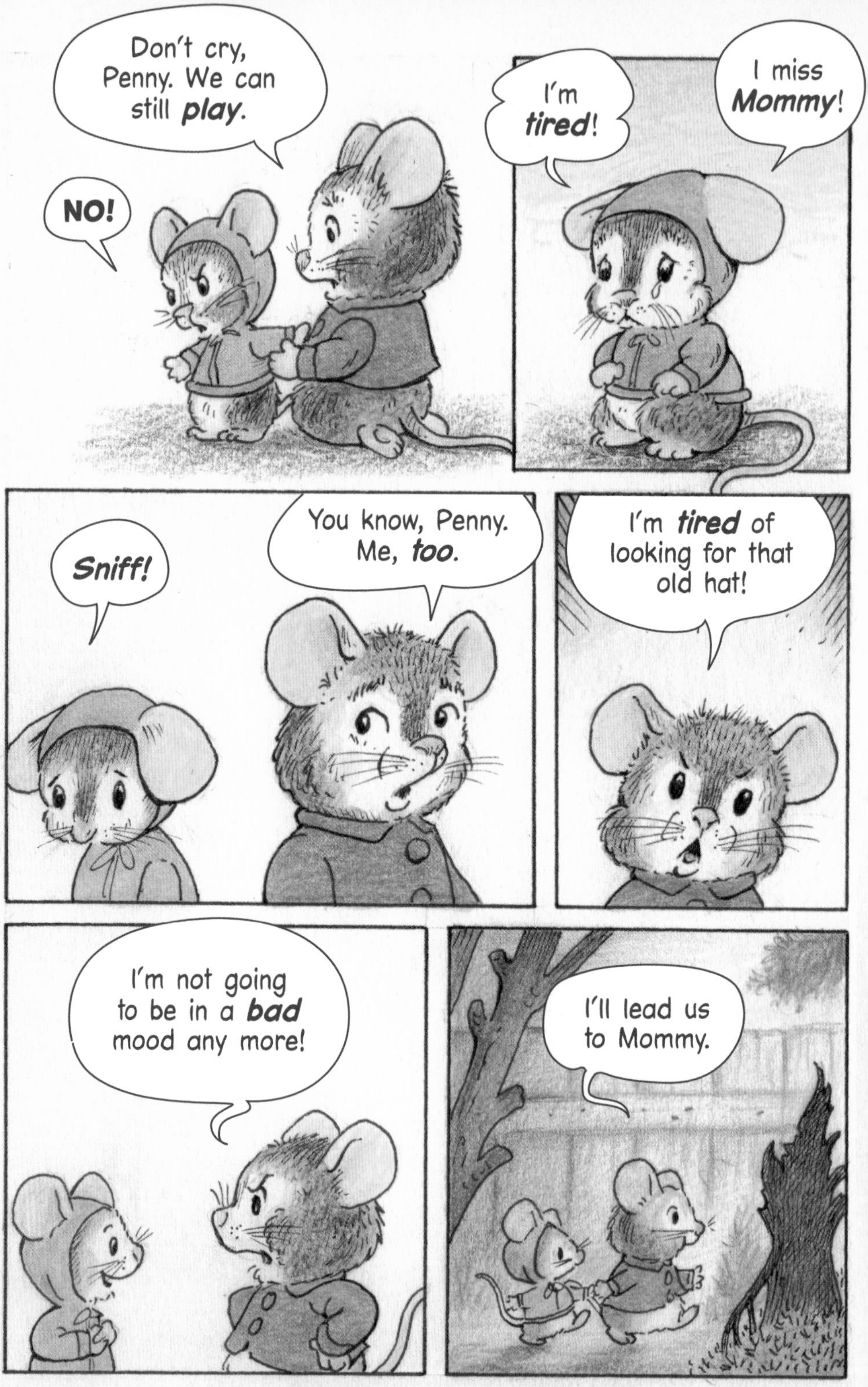
Don't cry, Penny. We can still *play*.
NO!
I'm *tired*!
I miss *Mommy*!
Sniff!
You know, Penny. Me, *too*.
I'm *tired* of looking for that old hat!
I'm not going to be in a *bad* mood any more!
I'll lead us to Mommy.

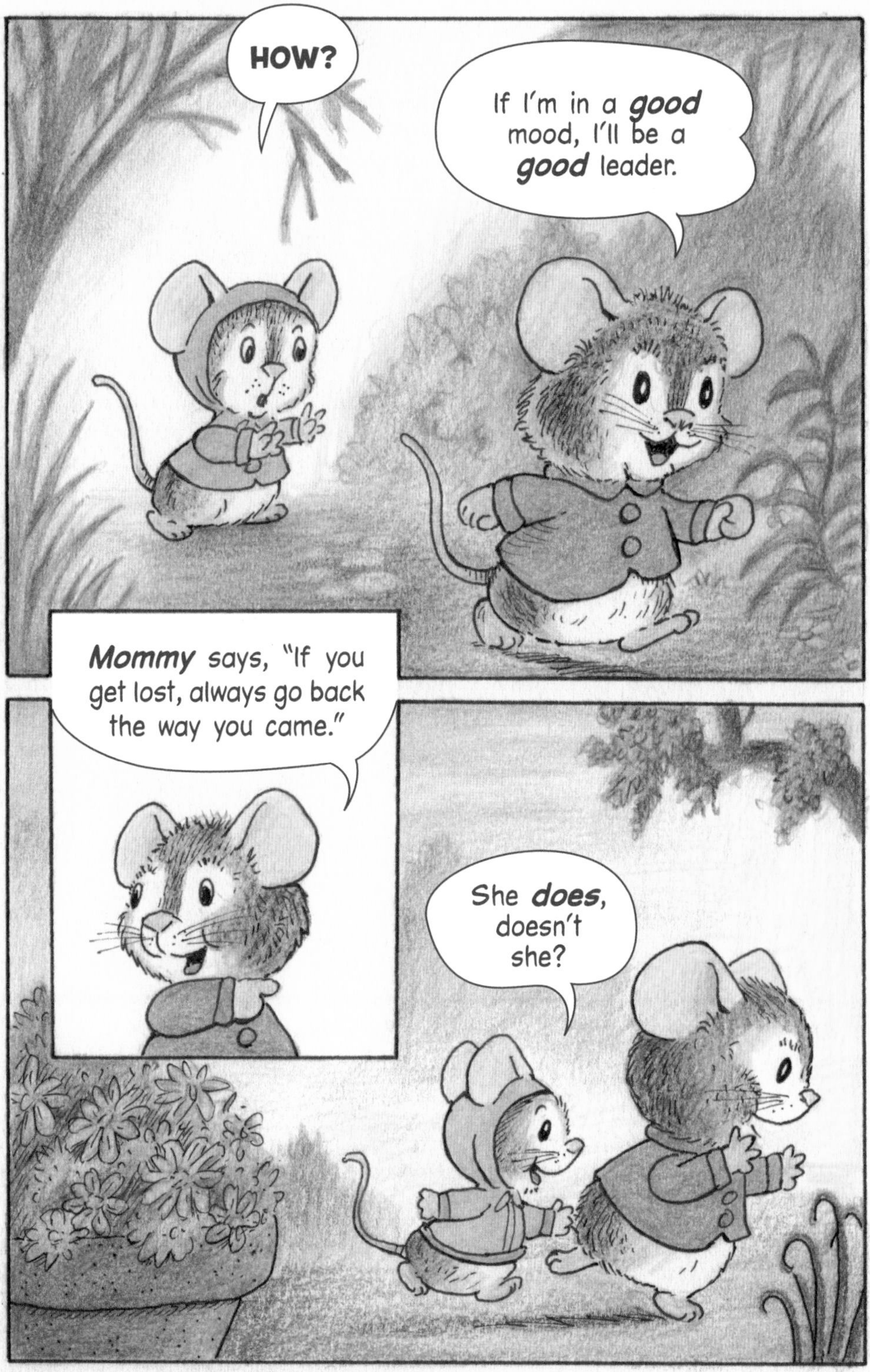
HOW?
If I'm in a *good* mood, I'll be a *good* leader.
Mommy says, "If you get lost, always go back the way you came."
She *does*, doesn't she?

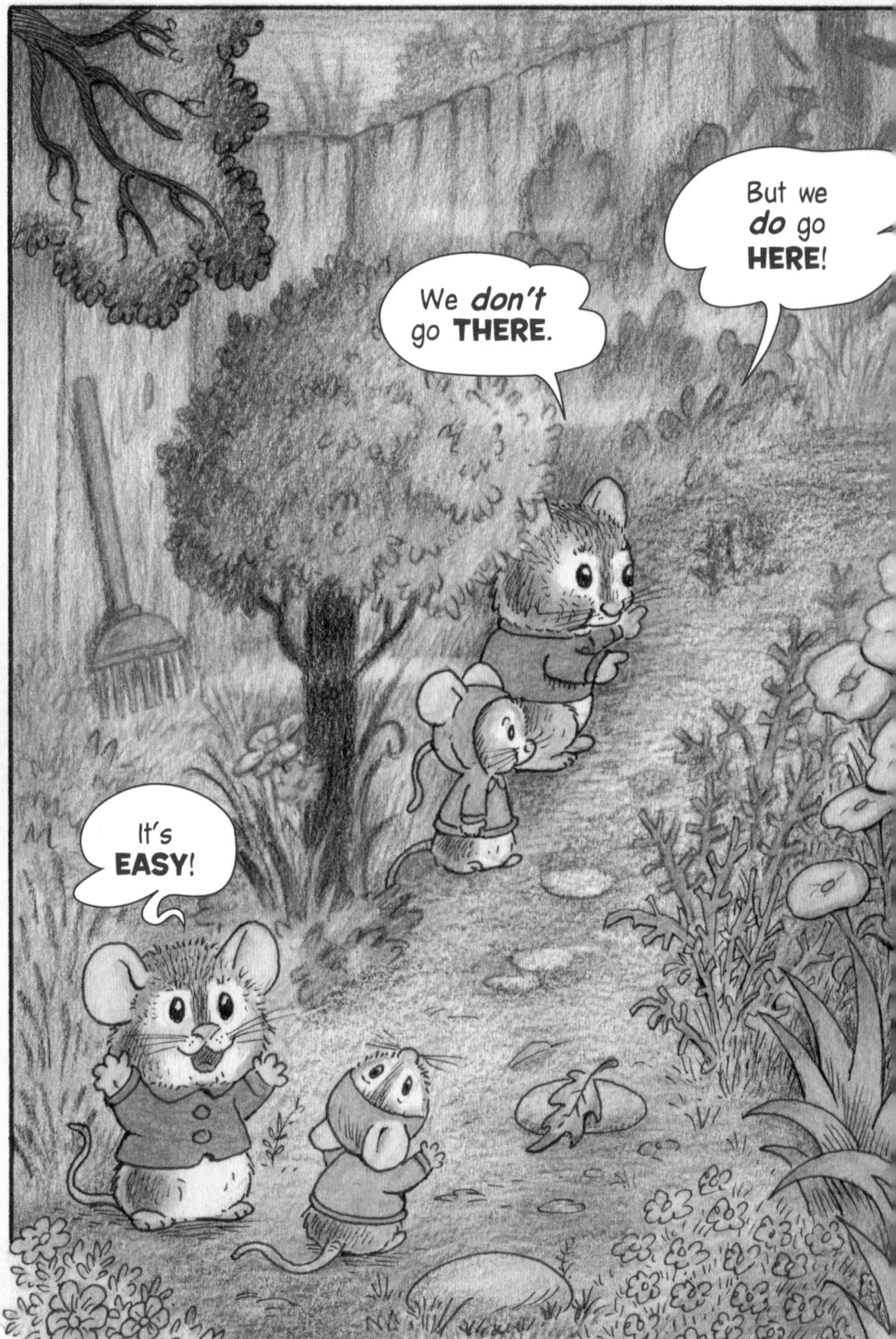
But we **do** go **HERE**!
We **don't** go **THERE**.
It's **EASY**!

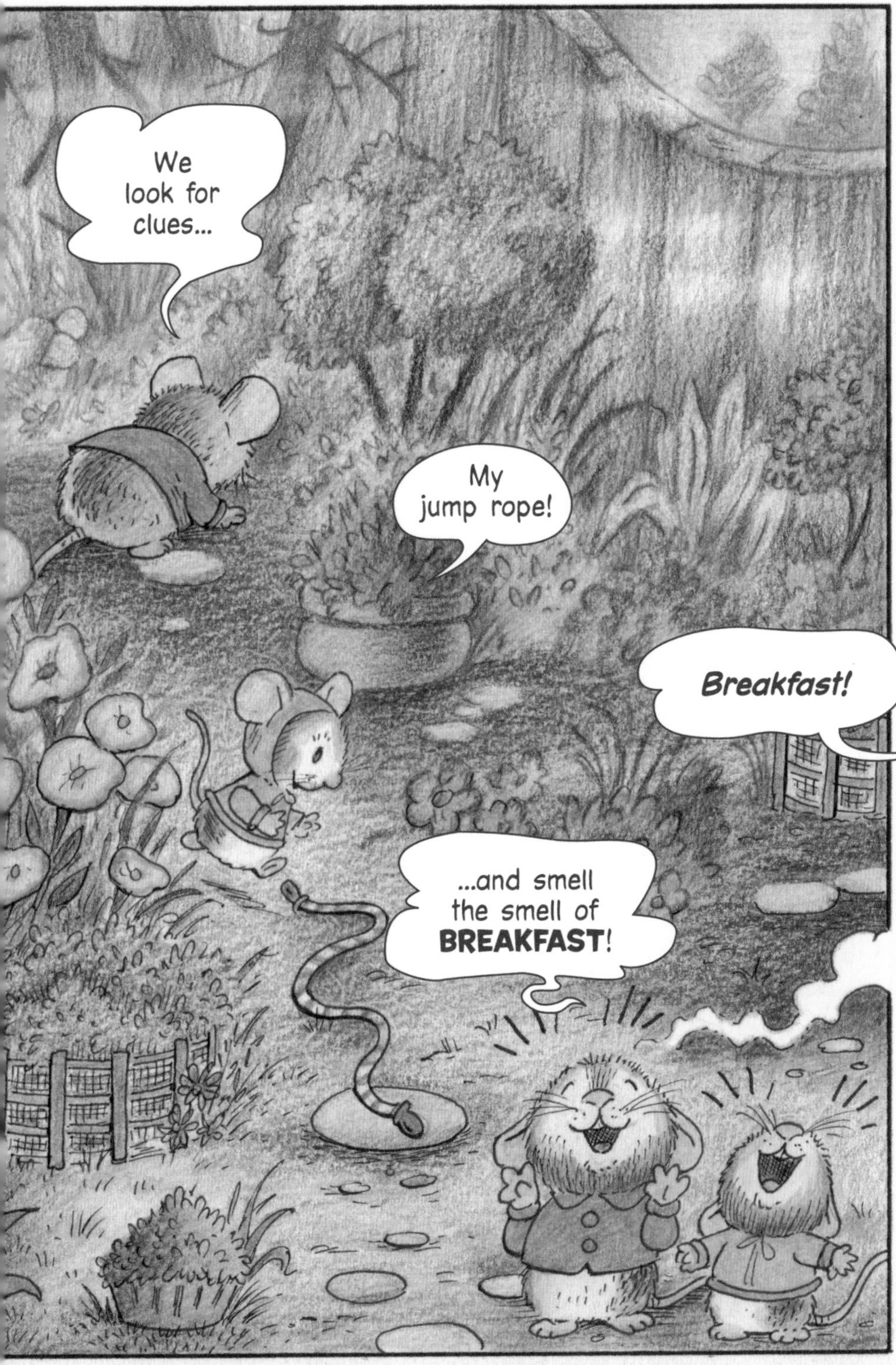
We look for clues...
My jump rope!
Breakfast!
...and smell the smell of **BREAKFAST**!

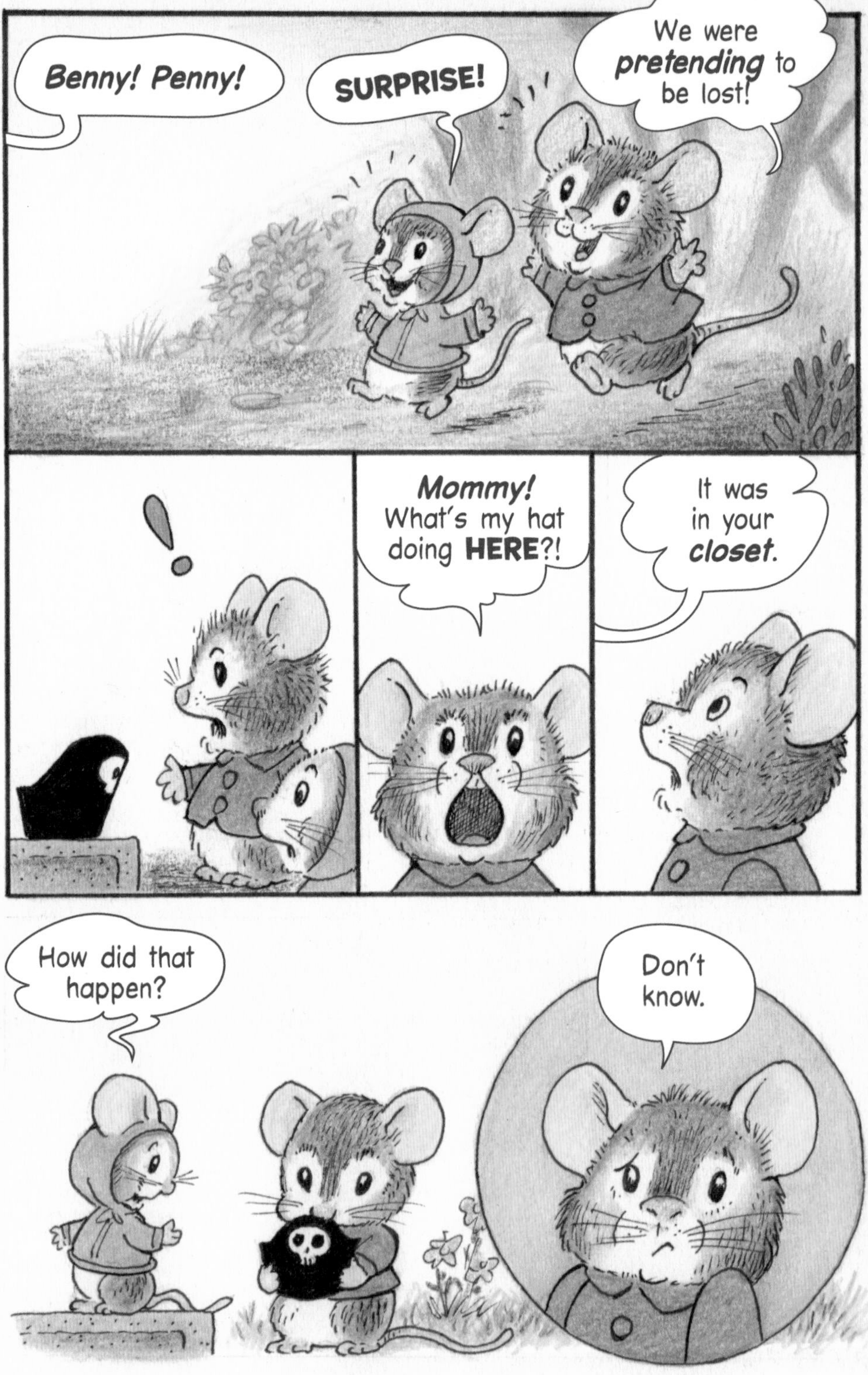
Benny! Penny!
SURPRISE!
We were *pretending* to be lost!
!
Mommy! What's my hat doing **HERE**?!
It was in your *closet*.
How did that happen?
Don't know.

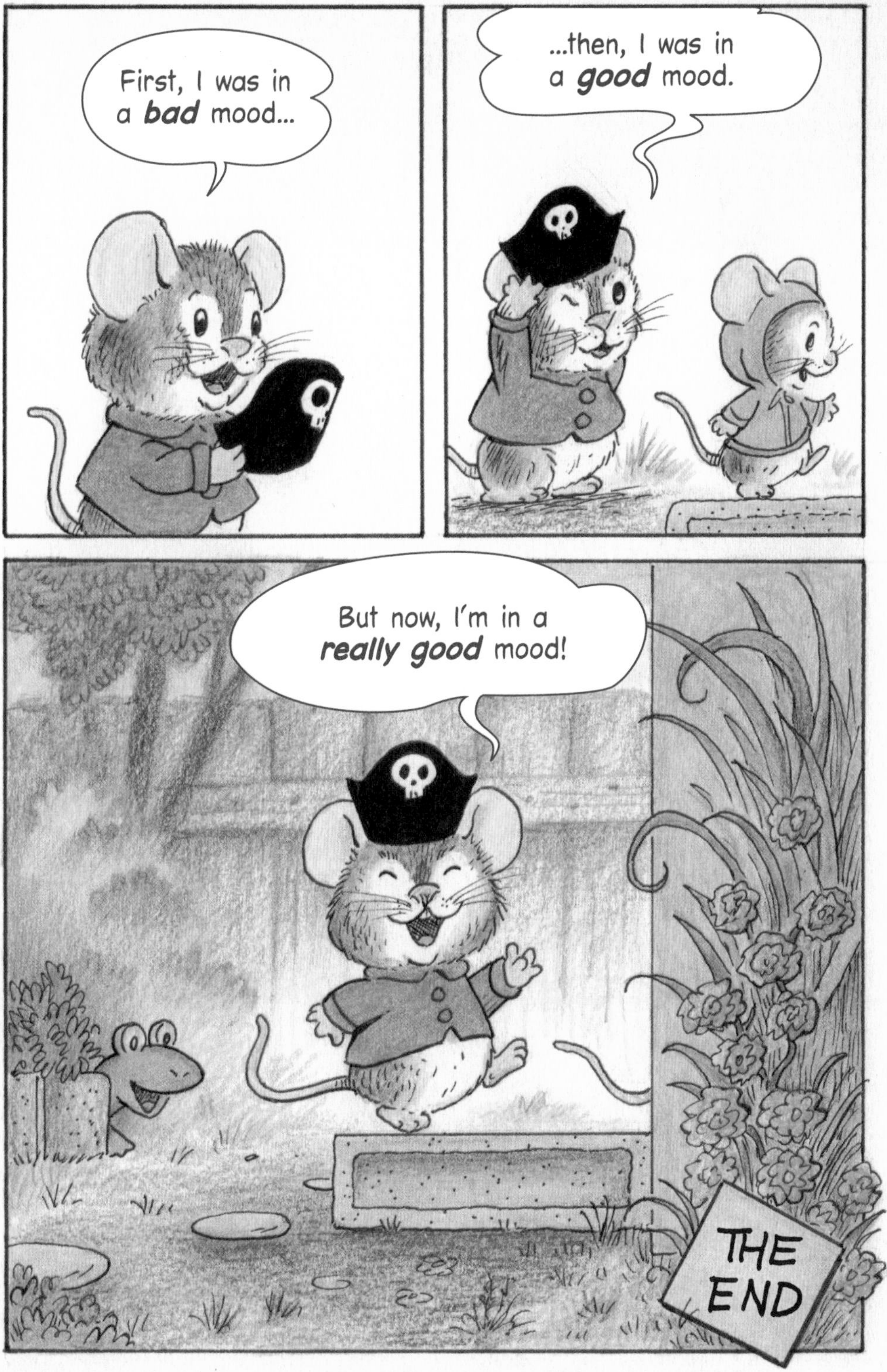
First, I was in a **bad** mood...
...then, I was in a **good** mood.
But now, I'm in a **really good** mood!
THE END

ABOUT THE AUTHOR

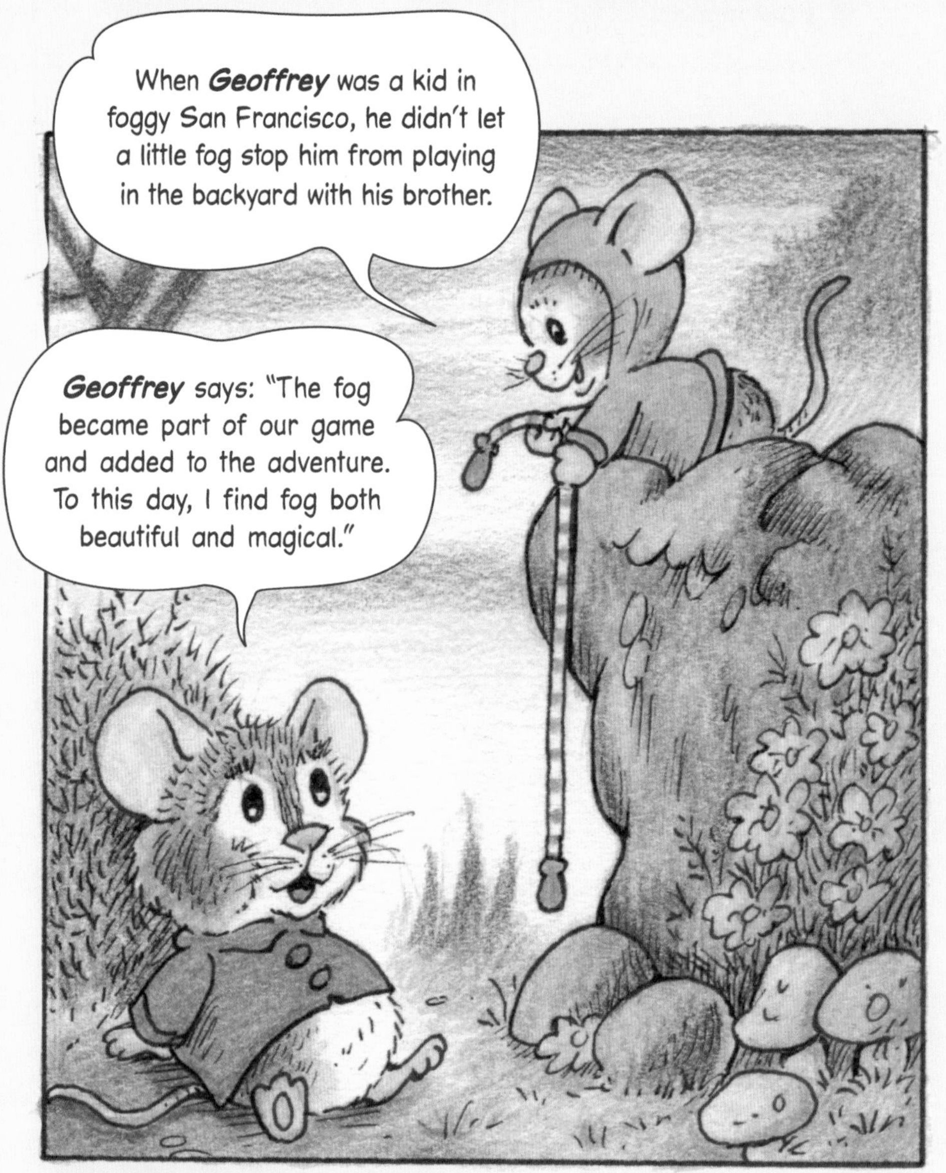
When *Geoffrey* was a kid in foggy San Francisco, he didn't let a little fog stop him from playing in the backyard with his brother.
Geoffrey says: "The fog became part of our game and added to the adventure. To this day, I find fog both beautiful and magical."

GEOFFREY HAYES is the author/illustrator of the Patrick Brown books and of the successful series of early readers Otto and Uncle Tooth. His best-selling TOON Books series, Benny and Penny, has garnered multiple awards including the Theodor Seuss Geisel Award, given to "the most distinguished American book for beginning readers published during the preceding year."

HOW TO "TOON INTO READING"
in a few simple steps:

Our goal is to get kids reading—and we know kids LOVE comics. We publish award-winning early readers in comics form for elementary school, and present them in three levels.

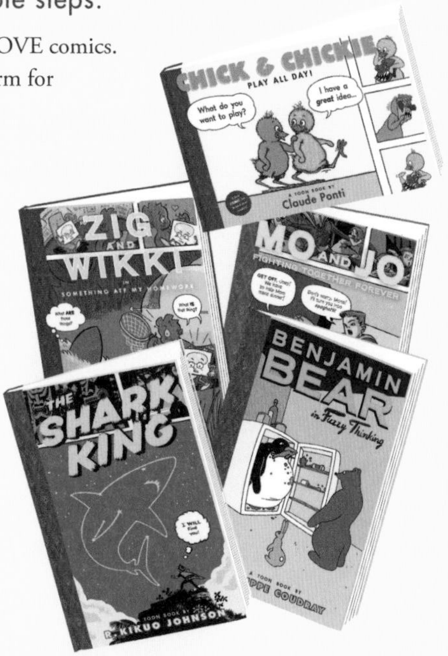
CHICK & CHICKIE
PLAY ALL DAY!
What do you want to play?
I have a great idea...
A TOON BOOK BY
Claude Ponti
ZIG AND WIKKI
MO AND JO
FIGHTING TOGETHER FOREVER
BENJAMIN BEAR
in Fuzzy Thinking
THE SHARK KING
R. KIKUO JOHNSON

① FIND THE RIGHT BOOK

Veteran teacher Cindy Rosado tells what makes a good book for beginning and struggling readers alike: "A vetted vocabulary, plenty of picture clues, repetition, and a clear and compelling story. Also, the book shouldn't be too easy—or the reader won't learn, but neither should it be too hard—or he or she may get discouraged."

The TOON INTO READING!™ program is designed for beginning readers and works wonders with reluctant readers.

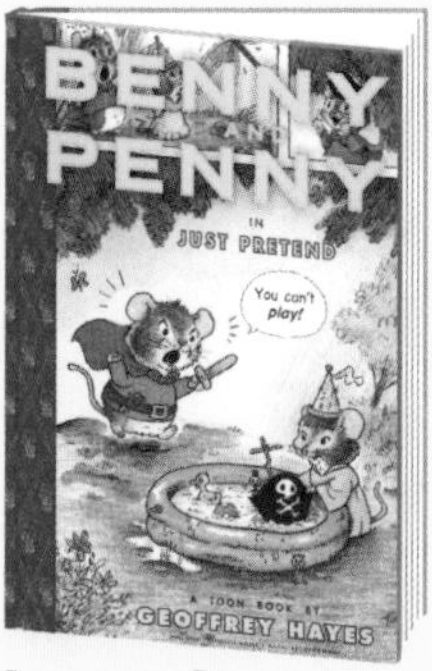
BENNY AND PENNY IN JUST PRETEND
You can't play!
A TOON BOOK BY
GEOFFREY HAYES

BENNY AND PENNY in Just Pretend

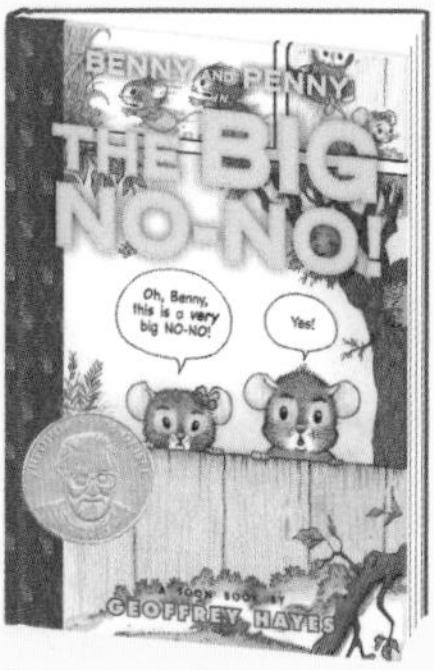
BENNY AND PENNY
THE BIG NO-NO!
Oh, Benny, this is a very big NO-NO!
Yes!
A TOON BOOK BY
GEOFFREY HAYES

BENNY AND PENNY in The Big No-No!

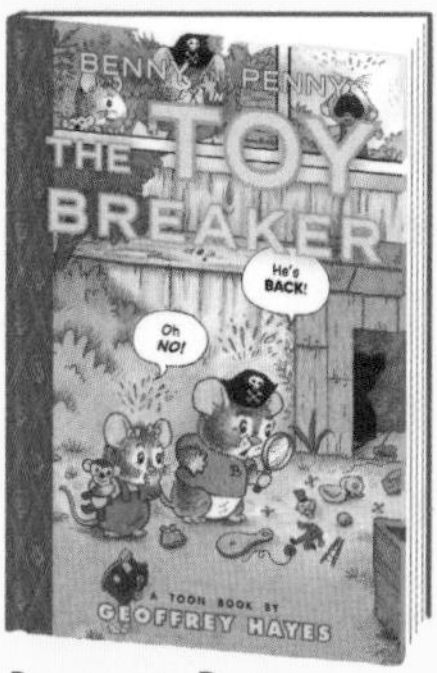
BENNY AND PENNY
THE TOY BREAKER
He's BACK!
Oh NO!
A TOON BOOK BY
GEOFFREY HAYES

BENNY AND PENNY in The Toy Breaker

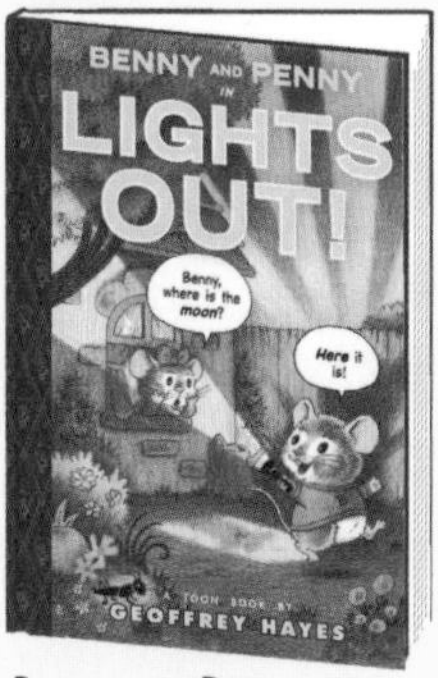
BENNY AND PENNY IN
LIGHTS OUT!
Benny, where is the moon?
Here it is!
A TOON BOOK BY
GEOFFREY HAYES

BENNY AND PENNY in Lights Out!

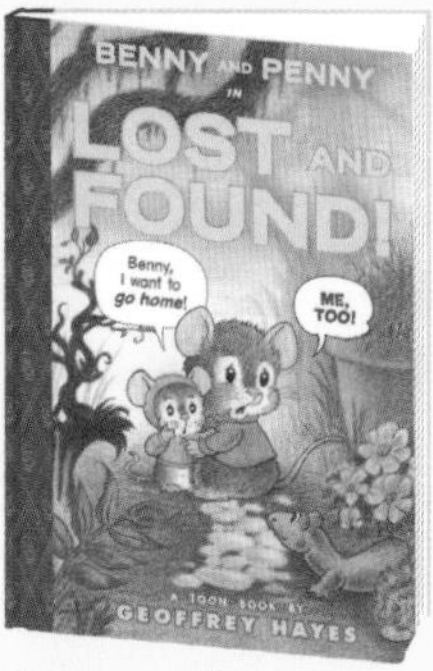
BENNY AND PENNY IN
LOST AND FOUND!
Benny, I want to go home!
ME, TOO!
A TOON BOOK BY
GEOFFREY HAYES

BENNY AND PENNY in Lost and Found!

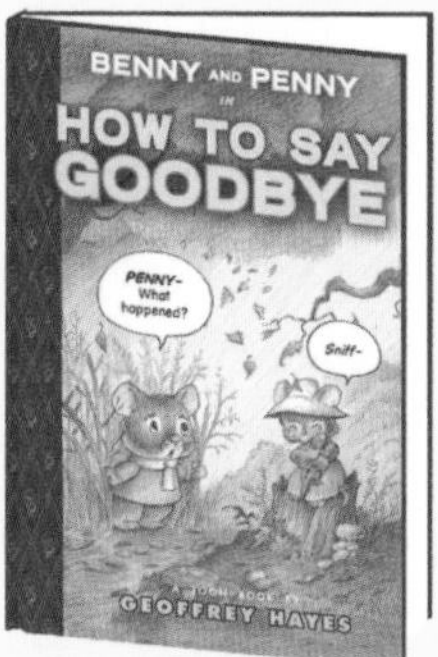
BENNY AND PENNY IN
HOW TO SAY GOODBYE
PENNY- What happened?
Sniff-
A TOON BOOK BY
GEOFFREY HAYES

BENNY AND PENNY in How to Say Goodbye

Look for these other Benny & Penny books by Geoffrey Hayes

2 GUIDE YOUNG READERS

What works?

Keep your fingertip <u>below</u> the character who's speaking.

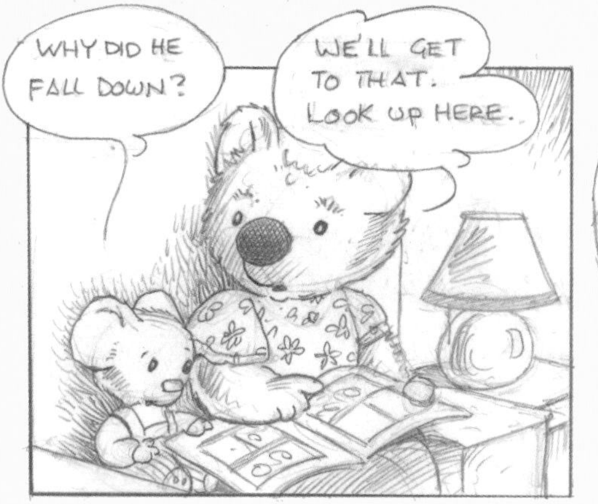
WHY DID HE FALL DOWN?
WE'LL GET TO THAT. LOOK UP HERE.

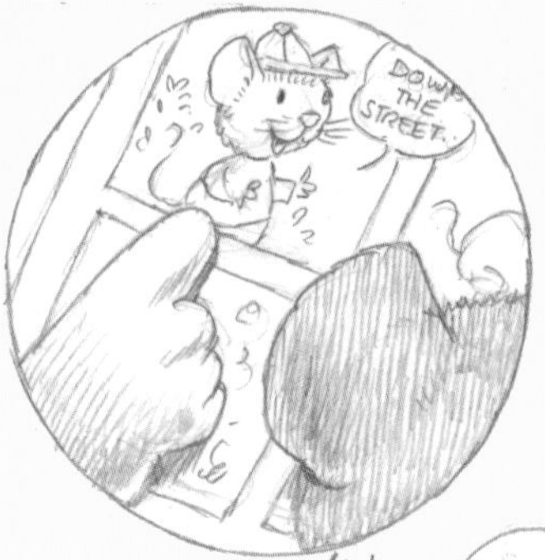

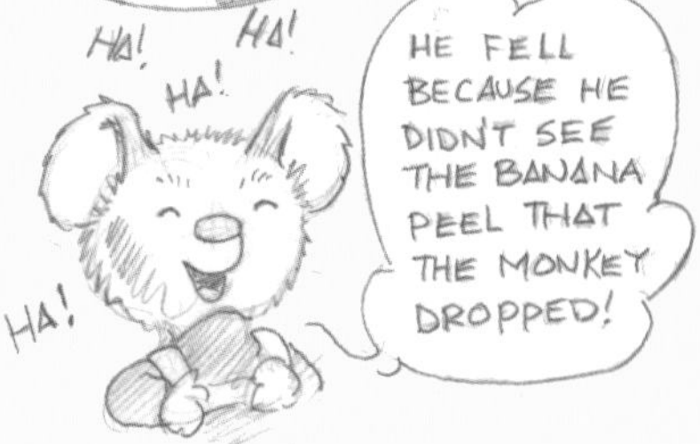
HA!
HA!
HA!
HA!
HE FELL BECAUSE HE DIDN'T SEE THE BANANA PEEL THAT THE MONKEY DROPPED!

3 LET THE PICTURES TELL THE STORY

In a comic, you can often read the story even if you don't know all the words. Encourage young readers to tell you what's happening based on the facial expressions and body language.

4 GET OUT THE CRAYONS

Kids see the hand of the author in a comic and it makes them want to tell their own stories. Encourage them to talk, write and draw!

Get kids talking, and you'll be surprised at how perceptive they are about pictures.

5 LET THEM GUESS

Comics provide a great deal of context for the words, so let young readers make informed guesses, and don't over-correct. In this panel, the artist shows a pirate ship, two pirate hats, and two pirate flags the first time the word "PIRATE" is introduced.

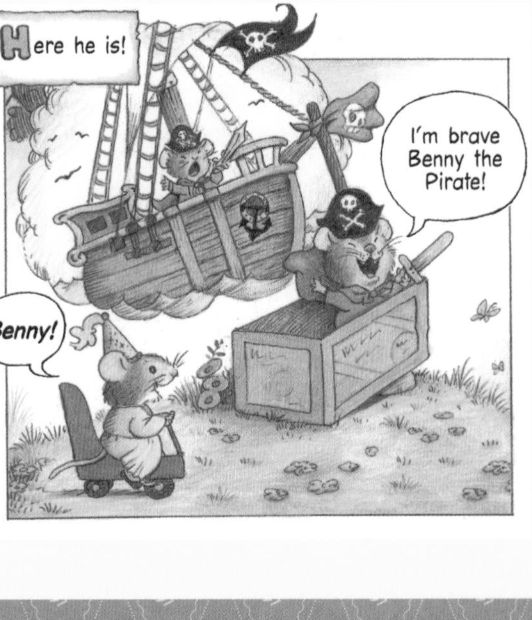
Here he is!
I'm brave Benny the Pirate!
Benny!